HARLEQUIN®
Presents

What do you love most about reading Harlequin Presents books? From what you tell us, it's our sexy foreign heroes, exciting and emotionally intense relationships, generous helpings of pure passion and glamorous international settings that bring you pleasure!

Welcome to February 2007's stunning selection of eight novels that bring you emotion, passion and excitement galore, as you are whisked around the world to meet men who make love in many languages. And you'll also find your favorite authors: Penny Jordan, Lucy Monroe, Kate Walker, Susan Stephens, Sandra Field, Carole Mortimer, Elizabeth Power and Anne McAllister.

Sit back and let us entertain you....

Dinner ^{at}8

Don't be late!

He's suave and sophisticated,

He's undeniably charming.

And, above all, he treats her like a lady.

Beneath the tux, there's a primal passionate
lover, who's determined to make her his!

Wined, dined and swept away by a
British billionaire!

Elizabeth Power

TAMED BY
HER HUSBAND

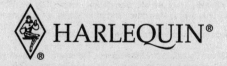

HARLEQUIN®

TORONTO • NEW YORK • LONDON
AMSTERDAM • PARIS • SYDNEY • HAMBURG
STOCKHOLM • ATHENS • TOKYO • MILAN • MADRID
PRAGUE • WARSAW • BUDAPEST • AUCKLAND

ISBN-13: 978-0-373-12609-5
ISBN-10:   0-373-12609-3

TAMED BY HER HUSBAND

First North American Publication 2007.

Copyright © 2005 by Elizabeth Power.

This edition published by arrangement with Harlequin Books S.A.

® and TM are trademarks of the publisher. Trademarks indicated with ® are registered in the United States Patent and Trademark Office, the Canadian Trade Marks Office and in other countries.

www.eHarlequin.com

Printed in U.S.A.

All about the author...
Elizabeth Power

ELIZABETH POWER was born in Bristol,
where she still lives with her husband in a
300-year-old cottage. A keen reader, as a teenager
she had already made up her mind to be a
novelist. But it wasn't until a few weeks before
her thirtieth birthday that Elizabeth was thinking
about what she had done with her first thirty
years and realized she had been telling herself
she would "start writing tomorrow" for at least
twelve of them and took up writing seriously.
Within two weeks the letter that was to change
her life arrived from Harlequin. *Rude Awakening*
was to be published in 1986. After a prolonged
absence, Elizabeth is pleased to be back at her
keyboard again, and with new romances already
in the works.

Of her writing, emotional intensity is paramount
in her books. She says, "Times, places and trends
change, but emotion is timeless." A powerful
story line with maximum emotion set in a
location in which you can really live and breathe
while the story unfolds is what she strives for.
Good food and wine come high on her list of
priorities, and what better way to sample these
delights than by just having to take another trip
to some new exotic resort. Oh, and of course to
find a location for the next book!

CHAPTER ONE

HE COULD feel the tension in the air. The thick heat of the late afternoon was oppressive and, even in his lightweight suit, Kane Falconer felt decidedly uncomfortable.

Normally, Barcelona was a place in which he liked to linger, but now, striding through the tree-lined, pedestrian thoroughfare, past the stalls with their souvenirs and bright floral displays and the open-air cafés, he was glad his business was over.

The student protest march in which he had very little interest, had brought the city to a standstill. In the surrounding streets, horns blared, throttles revved, with the lurid Spanish phrases being hurled from dusty cabs adding to the noise pollution. A squawking from one of the stalls grazed his already raw nerves, drawing his reluctant gaze to some brightly feathered creatures, caged, ready for sale, their fluttering wings ineffectual in the cramped confines of their environment.

Kane looked away in disgust and longed for his own space. At least he could walk away. He wasn't trapped here in this noise and heat and dust, he thought gratefully, already sensing mounting vibes of unease. He cast a glance towards the bright blooms of a basket decorating one of the stalls, his gaze falling on the girl who was standing on tiptoe, head thrown back as she inhaled one of the hanging blossoms.

The pale cascade of her hair moved like honey against her arched back, the striking length of that oh, so elegant neck bringing him up short with a swift, sharp stab of recognition.

Shannon Bouvier! Of all the places in all the towns in all the world, he hadn't expected to find her here.

When he had enquired at the address he had been given for

her in Milan over six months ago, he had been told by a rather surly landlord that she had left to move in with her boyfriend—that the two of them had gone abroad—but no one could tell him where.

Shannon Bouvier. Society girl. Rich bitch—as those less kindly disposed were apt to call her. Heiress to a national development company she neither wanted nor cared about.

She was thinner, he noted from an assessing glance over her clinging red crop-top and low-slung, rather shabby combat trousers—much thinner than when he had seen her last. Her features were almost gaunt compared with those of the blooming teenager who had kept her dignity—if not her reputation—under the claws of the mauling British Press—but it was definitely her.

His jaw was set in a determined cast, his body tense from an awareness he didn't want to acknowledge as he steeled himself to close the distance between them.

Shannon took the pale orchid the elderly stall-keeper handed her—a gesture the Spanish woman had taken to making often when the 'fragile-looking *señorita*', as she called her, passed her stall.

Now the woman shrugged, her arms thrown wide at all the shouting and horn-blowing induced by the marchers. It was supposed to be a peaceful demonstration, but some dissidents had threatened to disrupt it, Shannon remembered uneasily, flicking a glance over her shoulder towards the advancing students. She gasped at the sight of the man blocking her view.

'Hello, Shannon.'

Something leapt inside her, that familiar excitement she had always felt in his presence coupled with something else which instantly put her on her guard. He was the last person she had expected to see. Yet here he was, as large as life.

No, larger than life, she thought hectically, as his dark and dominating presence seemed to put everything else out of focus so that he became the only noticeable person in Las Ramblas, and the demonstration gaining momentum down the surging thoroughfare was like the backdrop to a movie. Unreal. Only secondary to what was going on between the two of them.

'Kane!' If she had wanted to appear unfazed, then that shocked little utterance would have denied her even that simple pleasure. Too long, it seemed, her eyes rested on his hard-boned face, reacquainting her with every well-remembered feature; the thick, expertly cut brown hair, the high forehead and firmly-set square jaw; that distinctive and tantalising cleft in his chin. 'What are you doing here?'

From the pale tailored suit that accentuated the hard fitness of his body, he was obviously there on business, although he was tie-less and his fine white shirt was unbuttoned at the neck, offering a glimpse of tanned flesh beneath the corded strength of his throat.

'I was about to ask you the same thing.' Above the blaring horns and angry voices his tone was soft and deep—relaxed. He didn't seem tense or agitated as she was, left wondering what to say. 'I thought you'd gone much farther afield.' Assessingly, his eyes seemed to scour the delicate lines of her face, touched briefly on the equally delicate perfection of the orchid she was holding. 'Someone told me you were in Rio.'

Had they? Mentally, Shannon dragged herself from the mesmerising effects of those blue-grey eyes. Had he been discussing her? Or had it been just a casual comment on someone else's part? A careless reference to the girl who wrecked lives, who had made the headlines for a few days nearly three years ago, providing sustenance for a scandal-loving public?

'Well…as you can see…' she gave a careless laugh—threw out her arms '…I'm not.' Then wished she hadn't when the action drew the man's attention to the swell of her small breasts beneath the scarlet crop-top with its logo emblazoned across it: *Emancipation for Bulls.*

His mouth—a cruel mouth, she had always thought—firmed, and those steely eyes looked, as they had often looked—as though they were mocking her. Except that they hadn't the last time. 'Still fighting the cause of the underdog, Shannon?'

She didn't even glance down. 'Someone has to.'

His mouth moved again, a twist of lips that was somewhere between a grimace and a smile. 'I veer towards the view that if you're a guest in someone else's country, you respect their customs.'

With a dignity she hoped she was managing to hang on to, she lifted her chin and said quietly, 'You're entitled to your view.'

His head dipped briefly, leaving her feeling like someone who had just won a round merely because their opponent had let them. 'So what *are* you doing here in Spain?'

She glanced across at a young couple browsing through the handcrafted jewellery on one of the adjacent stalls. What was she doing here?

About to tell him, she thought better of it and, with a small shrug, uttered, 'Killing time.' Well, it was the truth—of sorts.

The amusement went out of the hard masculine face and his mouth took on a decidedly grim line. 'What the hell's that supposed to mean?'

Shannon tensed, catching the disapproval in those dangerously soft tones. But then, he had always disapproved. Just like everyone else with his preconceived ideas about her. And no more so than that last time, when he had called her an attention-seeking little socialite. Surprisingly, the memory still hurt.

'I mean it's as good a place as any to do nothing.' To get over things. Recharge one's batteries, she thought. To get well.

'Is that what you're doing?' He slipped a hand into his trouser pocket, stretching the fabric across hips that were lean and hard. 'Nothing?' The disdain on his lips assured her he wasn't too impressed with her answer.

She shrugged again, a careless gesture saying nothing—expressing everything. Everything he would expect from her, she thought bitterly.

Out of the corner of her eye, she saw the woman behind the flower stall studying them both, weighing them up, obviously considering them an item. The tall, dynamic-looking man and the equally tall blonde girl. She wondered if everyone considered them a couple; wondered if they could sense that underlying current of electricity that charged the air between them, a sexually charged awareness that had always been there—albeit unacknowledged by either of them—even before Kane had stormed out of her father's office for good, refusing, unlike the other members of the board, to bend to Ranulph Bouvier's will.

'Where are you staying?' Even as he asked it, Kane felt the tension building inside him, a tension every bit as keen as that that he sensed boiling around them.

The district she named was impressive, but he wouldn't have expected anything less.

'On holiday?'

Almost imperceptibly she appeared to hesitate before shaking her head.

'Are you here alone?' As his eyes roved over that gaunt, yet strikingly beautiful face, she seemed to be making her own silent assessment of his motives for asking.

'Yes.'

So the boyfriend hadn't lasted. 'Now, why doesn't that surprise me?'

'I don't know. Why doesn't it?'

God! She was confident! What was she now? he wondered. Twenty-one? But then, even as a gangling adolescent she had

had more poise than some women twice her age. He was surprised to realise how vividly he could remember that.

'You have an apartment here?'

'A house,' she corrected. 'It belongs to a friend of mine.'

'I see.'

'No, you don't,' she returned, hating his derogatory tone.

No, he didn't, he thought, wondering why she was so shabbily dressed, wondering what had happened to her. But he didn't want to pursue the point—didn't want to discover, to his own unexpected annoyance, that there was a boyfriend after all.

'So what happens when you've grown tired of doing nothing in Barcelona?' His words were scathing. 'Or isn't that very likely?'

'It's likely.' In contrast her tone was light, deliberately careless.

'When?' he asked roughly. 'When something—or *someone*—more exciting comes along?'

Beneath the soft fabric of her top, Shannon's chest lifted with the effort of stopping herself from throwing some caustic response right back at that arrogant, handsome face. She could feel the latent anger beneath that cool, imperturbable exterior, which she could see no reason for. She had been a fool and she had paid for it. But that was all in the past, so why did he seem hell-bent on constantly reminding her of it?

Now, in answer to his remark about something exciting coming along, she murmured, 'It usually does,' refusing to let him see through the invisible barrier she had erected around herself, to see the real Shannon Bouvier.

'And have you never given any thought to the fact that your father might be wondering where his only daughter has got to?' Through the seething noise around them his question came hard and disparaging. 'Just once considered giving some thought to going home?'

Pain vied with the anger his judgemental tone gave rise to,

a keen, cutting emotion she fought to suppress. Because, of course, she dreamed of nothing else. But Ranulph Bouvier had made it all too clear after that scandal she'd been involved in what he expected of his only daughter—and it wasn't a life she wanted. She had more self-esteem leading the life she had been leading for the past two and a half years—of which people like Kane Falconer knew absolutely nothing—than she had under the weight of her father's controlling millions.

'No, Kane. I haven't. And I don't really think it's any concern of yours, do you?'

'With not a word about how he is? How things are back in England?'

A swift surge of anxiety darkened the bright blue of Shannon's eyes. At first she had kept tabs on how things were at home, reading papers, pumping for information anyone who might be remotely connected with the company, with her father. But that was some time ago now, and for the past few months she hadn't exactly been in a position to go chasing information…

Tentatively, she asked, 'Have you been in touch with him?' If he had, then it would surprise her. From the way he had thrown up his job and the company, there had been no love lost between him and Ranulph Bouvier—no going back.

'Forget it,' he rasped. 'As you said, what you do is none of my business.' He slipped his other hand in his pocket, glancing over his shoulder at the pedestrian-packed thoroughfare, his jaw set like the hard, grim face of a rock.

He had wanted to say more. He could feel the words choking him as the traffic was choking the streets, because the marchers were at the top of La Rambla now. He could hear them chanting, people shouting, fuelling the aggravation produced by the demonstrators, and he had to raise his own voice to make himself heard.

'What *is* this all in aid of?' It was a rhetorical question. He had already asked it of the MD at the meeting earlier, a satisfactory conclusion of negotiations that had secured him the development of further luxury apartments along the Côte d'Azur.

'They want fairness. Understanding,' she answered quietly.

Was she appealing to him for those things? he wondered. Was that why she was looking at him as if he was some inexorable tyrant, because she thought he was treating her unfairly? Failing to understand her? The combination of her husky voice with her fair and fragile loveliness was touching the most elemental core of his masculinity, stirring him to the angry realisation that he was no less affected by her than every other man she must have known. Oh, he understood all right! Understood that Ranulph Bouvier was killing himself over the loss of his only child, while his self-centred, pleasure-seeking daughter was jet-setting round the world, enjoying herself, looking—as she had just admitted herself—solely for excitement. And yet when he had mentioned her going home, he could almost imagine he had seen pain beneath the rebellion in those baby-blue eyes…

'Perhaps they're going the wrong way about it,' he declared loudly over the din. 'They're hardly likely to engender sympathy by stopping tired people getting home from work.'

Patches of colour suffused the pale yet flawless skin across her cheekbones. 'Nor will they if they lie down and put up with everything the establishment dishes out!'

As she had refused to do? The thought rose unbidden in his mind, because, however she had behaved, there was no doubt that Ranulph Bouvier had ruled her with a will of iron, as he did everyone under him—his household staff, his work colleagues, his management. And, looking at the slender girl who stirred him in ways he was ashamed to admit to, and whose rebellious nature seemed too strong for her worryingly fragile appearance, he couldn't help but understand how smothered she must have felt by it.

'I'm surprised you aren't there—' Kane's chin jerked upwards '—leading the procession.'

'I might have been, only I had—' Her attention was distracted by something farther along the street.

Kane followed her gaze to where a group of young men were shouting and pushing one another outside one of the cafés.

'Only you had what?' he prompted, and then, unable to hold back the derision, 'Something more *exciting* to do?'

For a few seconds those blue eyes of hers seemed to darken—impale him. 'Yes, that's right,' she returned with a defiant toss of her head, her smile artificially sweet. 'I was—'

Something shot past them at shoulder level; an empty cola can, falling onto the ground behind her with a hollow clatter. It sent flares of danger shooting through Kane's blood.

'I think it's time we got out of here,' he urged.

Surprisingly, though, she shrugged away the hand clutching her elbow. 'I don't think I need—' she started to say, but her sentence was punctuated by a small cry as a piece of jagged wood glanced across her forehead. 'Ohh!'

As she crumpled, Kane's arm shot out around her bare middle. He couldn't contain the vehement little oath as he caught her, holding her upright. She felt as light as a sparrow against his own strength. 'Are you all right?'

For a few split seconds everything looked as squidgy as the liquid in a plastic water bottle.

'Shannon!' Kane's worried command fell hazily across her semi-dazed senses, like a shaft of light through a long, dark tunnel. She nodded and heard his heavily drawn sigh of relief.

'Now will you listen to me?' He sounded angry again, which was much more in keeping.

'Why are you angry? You're always angry with me.' The words escaped her as if she had had too much to drink. Perhaps, she thought, this was what they meant by punch-drunk.

'Shut up and walk. You can walk, can't you?'

'Of course I can walk,' she asserted as her spirits returned. What she didn't think she could do, though, was put up with the sensuous warmth of that soft-sleeved arm around her bare middle. It made her want to lean against him, let him take control, wallow in the comfort and protection he offered as the only link with home. 'I'm fine,' she breathed in protest, striving mentally and physically to liberate herself. Physically was easier.

'Come on, then,' he insisted, soundly oddly hoarse as he took her elbow again and, grabbing the grubby canvas shoulder bag she had dropped as she'd staggered, propelled her in front of him, away from the imminent danger zone.

'My orchid!'

She glanced back, saw it lying there, crushed and broken on the pavement.

'Leave it!' he ordered, and she felt the unexpected rush of foolish tears prick her eyes as he hustled her away.

At the end of the pedestrian thoroughfare, he was bundling her into a taxi.

'Why are we going to the marina?' she asked when he climbed in beside her, having heard him giving the driver their destination.

'Because I came in on the boat.' The car door slammed ominously shut behind him. 'You can rest aboard until all this chaos dies down.'

'The boat?' A pulse in Shannon's temples began to throb. What boat?

Seeing her frown, he smiled. 'A mixture of business and pleasure,' he told her as the taxi began nosing its way through the clogged street towards the harbour. 'Fortunately most of the business has been taken care of, for today at least.'

She didn't think she could handle this—being marooned with Kane Falconer in something so confining as a boat. Not that she was worried he would treat her with anything but his usual cool courtesy. It was just the unsettling intimacy that the whole thing implied.

'I really think I should try and get home,' she stressed, glancing anxiously back over her shoulder.

'And just how do you propose to do that? On the bus? Or are you hoping for a cab with wings to get you back through town?'

He'd obviously assumed—and correctly—that she didn't have her own transport. Her Porsche, like most of her possessions, had been left behind when she had fled England and the life she had been unable to face any more.

He had a point though, she thought, looking back again at the city's gridlocked traffic. The scene behind them had turned frightening and, back beyond the waterfront, not a vehicle was moving, every bus, coach and taxi stuck with private and commercial vehicles in one impossible jam.

'I can walk,' she said.

'With that bang on the head?' Incredulity laced his words. 'You feel up to that, do you?'

She wished she could say she did, but the truth was, she didn't.

'Why the rush?' he asked a little more gently when she didn't respond. 'Do you have some hungry pet waiting at home?'

'No.'

He laughed softly, sensing her lingering reluctance. 'Don't worry,' he advised. 'If you've got a date tonight, I'm sure we can get you back there before he thinks you've stood him up.'

'Thanks,' she snapped, averting her head so that the hot June sun shining through the open window played across the bright gold of her hair, accentuating the tense beauty of her profile.

'Have you?' he prompted suddenly.

'Have I what?'

'Got a date?'

Whatever his motive for asking, she was sure it wasn't for any magnanimous reason like helping her to keep it, and quietly she responded, 'I don't see that that's anything to do with you.'

They were crossing the bridge, the imposing monument of Columbus that dominated the skyline catching his attention for a moment.

'You're right, it isn't,' he said.

'Why did you ask, then?' she challenged and, wanting to throw him off balance, tagged on, 'Or was that an overture to asking me out yourself?'

He laughed then, a harsh, cynical sound that assured her of what he thought of that idea. He didn't have to say anything. After all, he had had ample opportunity to ask her in the past, and he never had.

Suddenly, feeling ridiculously desperate for his approval, she murmured, 'Believe it or not, Kane, even I stay at home sometimes to wash my hair.'

'Meaning?'

'I wasn't doing anything in particular.'

The look he shot her was one of pure scepticism, which just showed her how pointless it was, she thought, even trying to change his mind about her.

'Must be tough,' he observed, his mouth turning mocking, 'doing nothing all day and then having nothing to do all night.' His eyes were more serious now, uncomfortably assessing. 'I would have credited you with more intelligence than to drift around the world—as you admitted in your own words—"killing time".'

Would he? She looked at him quickly. Did he consider her intelligent? Worth something? That her life had some value? Something warming and utterly reckless stole along her veins.

'Who says I'm drifting round the world?'

'Aren't you?' he said grimly. And before she could answer,

'Life isn't all one whopping big party, Shannon. I'd hoped you would have learnt that by now.'

She glanced out of the window, biting her tongue to stop herself hurling back just how big a party life had been for her. A little way ahead, rows of countless masts pointed skywards from the bobbing dinghies in the marina; small sailing craft, moored alongside the gleaming hulls of more powerful motor vessels.

'Isn't it?' Hair stirring in the wind, she brought her attention back to him again. 'Maybe not for you, Kane, but, as we both know, I'm one of the privileged few. I've never been required to work. Daddy foots the bill for my every need through direct debit once a month—and I sleep late most days so I can get my kicks out of enjoying myself every night!'

Something in her outburst made him gravitate towards her, broad shoulders turning, mouth firming in disdain. He was altogether too big, too dominant and too disturbingly sexy, she thought with a tightness in her throat, noticing the way the soft fabric of his trousers pulled across his thighs as he breathed in a voice low enough so that their driver wouldn't hear, 'And am I supposed to be impressed by that?'

It was no good, she realised, despairing at the condemnation that glittered beneath those thick, dark lashes. Because, of course, she hadn't been trying to impress him, nor was any of it true. But the fact that he was so ready to believe the worst about her only fuelled her determination to let him.

'Go to hell,' she murmured, turning away.

In the marina, with Kane having paid off the taxi, Shannon shrugged aside the assistance he offered, making her own way beside him along the quay.

'Which is yours?' she quizzed sarcastically, glancing at some rustic-looking fishing tubs that made up the line of moored vessels, along with small masted craft and compact cabin cruisers, built for speed but with very little comfort.

She was lagging behind him, finding it increasingly difficult to match his stride.

He stopped beside one of the small cruisers, cutting an impressive figure against the sleek, gleaming lines of an ocean-going motor yacht that caught Shannon's attention just ahead of them, waiting for her to catch up.

Now, that would suit you more, Kane, she fantasised, dragging her weary eyes from what had to be over fifty feet of sporty-looking, unadulterated opulence. That's more your style. Fast. Powerful. Expensive.

'Are you all right?'

She had suddenly become the subject of his hard assessment and knew, as she drew level with him, that those shrewd eyes had seen the dampness that beaded her forehead, the way her chest was lifting a little too rapidly, making her breathing shallow.

'I'm fine.' She wasn't, though. She was feeling exhausted.

'Is it the bang on the head?'

'No, I'm OK,' she uttered, moving past him so as not to draw attention to herself. Just not as well yet as she had thought.

'Like hell!' he muttered, moving to catch her, lift her, and then, as if she were weightless, to step with her onto the gleaming yacht.

CHAPTER TWO

'YOU didn't have to carry me on,' she breathed, when he had made short work of the teak-laid steps to the covered aft deck and set her down in front of the yacht's sloping glass patio doors. 'I was perfectly capable of managing on my own.'

'Were you?' At the press of a button, the doors glided open on to an interior of pure luxury, cream leather settees contrasting with polished maple, soft carpeting complementing a ceiling panelled in suede. 'For one thing,' Kane said, ushering her down the few steps that gave the low-level saloon complete privacy from the quayside, 'you've been dazed. For another you looked on the verge of collapse. You're pale. You're dark under the eyes. On top of which, you're far too thin. In fact, you look an absolute wreck!'

'Thanks,' Shannon sent back over her shoulder with a rather pained grimace. 'Remind me to return the compliment sometime.'

He guided her up more carpeted steps into what comprised a beautifully appointed dinette and galley.

Back in the city, sirens wailed—police vehicles racing to control the disturbance.

'Sit down,' Kane commanded softly.

As much as she resented taking orders from him, in this instance Shannon was grateful to sink down onto the soft cream upholstery of the semicircular settee, rest her arms on the gleaming oval table around which it curved.

'I'm serious, Shannon. You look dreadful,' he reiterated, dumping her bag down on the table. 'What have you been doing for the past—what is it? Two, two and a half years?'

Censure burned in the eyes that raked disapprovingly over her. 'Playing too hard, as usual?'

Broodingly she watched him move around the marble-topped counter in the galley—as well-equipped as any modern kitchen—and fish for something in a cupboard before turning on one of the sparkling chrome taps over the sink.

'If you know, why ask?' she challenged, humouring him, because, after all, he knew it all, didn't he? 'I think it's called "burning the candle at both ends", but then you never do that, do you, Kane? Or are you just so big and strong that you can deflect all that hard living?' An involuntary glance over those broad shoulders and unquestionably fit physique made her blood race, increasing the ache at her temples as he strode back to her.

'Let's take a look at that,' he said, without answering her.

Disconcertingly, he caught her chin, his touch surprisingly gentle as he inspected the injury she had sustained to her forehead.

'The skin's not broken, but I don't think you'll escape without some bruising.' Deftly he applied a cold compress to the wound with the moistened lint he had taken from the cupboard, causing Shannon to suck in her breath.

'Does it hurt?'

'No,' she lied, not wanting him to think her feeble. But it wasn't only that. It was being this close to him, with the disturbing intimacy of his action that was making her pulse throb so hard that she wondered if he could hear it, so that, not trusting herself to look anywhere else, she kept her gaze fixed on the fine transparency of his shirt through his open jacket and the suggestion of dark body hair beneath it that spanned the hard contours of his chest.

'Do you actually *own* this thing?' she asked tightly, trying not to let him see how his tangible warmth and the subtlety of his cologne were affecting her as he gently bathed her wound. If he did own it, then he must have done very well for himself, she thought, since leaving Bouvier's.

'Would I be more of an interesting proposition for you if I said I did?'

Heat trickled through her and she felt her throat close over, even though his mocking tone assured her he was only toying with her. What respect did he have for her, after all? she reminded herself poignantly. Hadn't he condemned her along with all the rest?

'I wouldn't be tempted by you, Kane, if you had twenty yachts,' she returned with feigned sweetness, her artificial smile concealing pain—a deep, long-buried yearning. Her heart was beating too hard; much too fast. 'Anyway, don't you have a wife stowed away somewhere in one of those cabins?' A little jerk of her head indicated the steps she could see dipping down beside the helm, obviously leading to the vessel's sleeping quarters, while she racked her brain to remember whether he'd been seriously involved with anyone before.

'No wife,' he answered succinctly.

Relief was sweet and almost weakening. 'Why not?' she pressed and, trying to offset the feeling, 'You aren't getting any younger, you know.' What was he now? she asked herself. Thirty-three? Thirty-four?

'Keep still,' he commanded, without rising to her bait, so that suddenly she felt childish for making such a ridiculous statement. She'd always thought his maturity one of the most exciting things about him, and that hard sophistication had only increased with the years.

Plunged back into an enforced silence, she swallowed to ease the dryness in her throat, her eyes straying over his tight, lean waist and beyond.

Oh, heavens! she thought, deciding she would have more control over her reactions if she didn't have to look at him. She closed her eyes, then realised that his scent was even more acute, and that now she was even aware of his breathing. It was quite rapid, really—hard and shallow—as though carrying her hadn't been quite as effortless as she had thought.

'Here. You hold this.' His tone—his whole manner—as he surrendered the cold compress and moved away from her was surprisingly abrupt.

Kane was glad that he could busy himself with cups and saucers and filling a kettle. Touching Shannon Bouvier wasn't something that he—or any man, he was certain—could do imperviously. She affected him in ways he didn't want to be affected—in the profound and purely sensual way she had always affected him, he thought, if he was honest with himself—and silently he rebuked himself for the stirring he felt in his body. He'd be glad when the demonstration in town had broken up and he could take her home, he told himself, slamming a cupboard door, then wondering, as he spooned tea into a pot, why he felt an underlying reluctance to see her go. She didn't look well, and yet even her fragility lent itself to that mind-blowing sexuality of hers; did things to him that he knew weren't just the keen sense of the strong male to protect the weaker female, but stemmed from a less magnanimous, more primal desire to make this disastrously beautiful girl his. Because to lose oneself in a fatal submission to her lovely womanhood would be disastrous—and she was certainly a woman now, he recognised, that deceptively innocent look she had once had gone with the smouldering intensity of her full-blown sensuality. But for all that, she *wasn't* well. Anyone could see that, and he was concerned about her being in a strange country on her own. If she *was* on her own.

Damn it! Why did he have to get involved? he asked himself, gritting his teeth as he switched off the kettle and poured boiling water onto the fine-leaf tea. It wasn't as if he owed anything to Ranulph Bouvier, and even less to his pampered, self-indulgent daughter.

She wasn't his responsibility, he assured himself. He could just put her in a cab and let that take her back. She was over eighteen. She had chosen her life and it wasn't anything to do with him if she wanted to ruin it. So why did he feel this ridiculous and misplaced need to protect her?

'Does this thing have a bathroom?'

'Yes, it's…' Turning round as she was getting to her feet, he broke off, noticing how shaky, how drained she looked. Spaced out was the phrase that flew to his mind.

'Are you all right?' Coming around the counter, he could see the perspiration now dampening her forehead.

'Yes, I'm fine.' Her words, though, were slurred with fatigue. Or something else, he thought, feeling a sick fear suddenly grip him.

The way she looked. The gaunt features… Why hadn't he considered the possibility?

'Oh, no, you don't!' His hand clamped down on the scruffy canvas bag that, upon realising his intention, she had suddenly been making a grab for. He wouldn't put anything past this girl.

His fingers bit into the delicate bones of her wrists as he grasped them both, turning them over, subjecting each arm to his hard, critical inspection.

'What are you looking for?' Shocked anger sparked in her eyes before she tugged forcibly away from him. 'Signs of self-abuse?'

Without conscious thought, he was shaking out the contents of the bag onto the polished surface of the table.

'What the hell do you think you're doing?' she challenged, looking aghast.

He felt her heated indignation beating against him as he rifled through her things, and he hated himself for his actions, but he felt compelled to do it. For her sake. For her father's. For his…

Lipstick. Comb. Purse. Various papers. Bottle of tablets?

He picked it up to study the label, but swiftly she snatched the bottle away from him.

'An intestinal problem. All right? That's why I'm here and not Peru!'

His eyes narrowed questioningly. This girl sure got around. 'Peru?'

She shrugged. 'Rio. Peru. What does it matter to you? You're not interested in where I've been or what I might be doing. You're just worried about what I might be bringing onto your precious boat!'

That wasn't strictly true—in fact, not at all true—but he couldn't tell her that.

'So I was wrong.' He began dropping her belongings back into the bag, but she snatched that from him too.

'I suppose that's less of a climb-down than saying you're sorry!' Angry colour gave some glow to her cheeks as she began scooping up her possessions. 'I might not amount to much in your—or a lot of other people's—eyes, and basically I don't give a fig! But I do draw the line at—' her words were punctuated by short, angry breaths '—drugs, other people's husbands, and anything that puts me out of control! And I do happen to value my own body!'

As if that was a cue for them to do so, Kane's eyes slid, of their own volition, over her slender frame, coming to rest with a wave of heated awareness on the smooth flesh of her naked midriff, that small waist that most women would die for, that enviably flat stomach with its tantalising navel, the creamy camber of her hips. He wanted to coil his arm around her, draw her close as he had done when she had been struck back there on the Ramblas, only not to protect her this time, he realised shamefully, but to feel her warmth, the silky softness of her skin beneath his hands...

Blast her! He was thinking just like some smitten youth. He put a chastening clamp on his thoughts, picking up the small red document still lying on the table and handing it to her.

'Do you always carry your passport around with you?' That, too, was whisked from his hand to disappear with the rest of her things into the canvas holdall. 'I was burgled twice when I was…' She paused, looking at him as though weighing up what she was about to say. 'Anyway, ever since, I've kept it with me. Anyone who wants it will have to get past me first,' she told him determinedly, adding as a very pointed afterthought, 'and that includes you!'

Kane studied her with a dubious lift of an eyebrow. 'I'm sure you're strong enough to fend off anyone,' he commented wryly.

Her smile would have dazzled any man, but he wasn't fooled. She wasn't at all impressed by his remark.

'I don't think it would be a bad idea for you to lie down for a while,' he advised, bringing her below into the luxuriously appointed berth of the forward cabin with its pale lacquered furniture and queen-size bed. 'You look as though a bit of extra rest wouldn't do you any harm. And the shower…' He indicated the glass door leading off the bedroom. 'When you've freshened up, I'll bring you some tea.'

'Thanks.'

She looked like a waif, he thought, standing there in her shabby combats and little red top with that ridiculous slogan printed across it. Not like the heiress to a multimillion-pound concern whose difficulties she could have no concept of, and in which she certainly had no interest beyond the lifestyle it provided her with, he reminded himself with his jaw tightening. She might have been just some ordinary girl he had plucked off the street, if he hadn't known better—felt the deadly appeal in that dangerous vulnerability of hers that called to everything that was masculine in him…

'You said you drew the line.'

'What?' She pivoted round, startled. Obviously she thought he had already left.

'At other people's husbands,' he said softly.

She looked at him askance, some dark emotion crossing her lovely face, making him instantly regret having brought it up. Why had he? he wondered. To remind himself of just how dangerous she was? To protect himself? She was just a girl, for heaven's sake! What protection did he need?

'Yes.' She gave a careless shrug. 'Well, you know how the saying goes. Once bitten—twice shy.'

He couldn't help the quip that slipped from his lips. 'Is that why you asked if I was married, Shannon?'

As the cabin door clicked closed behind him, Shannon felt like throwing something at it. So she'd made a mistake. Been a poor judge of character. But why, oh, why, had Kane felt compelled to bring it up?

He was still treating her like the super-rich bitch the tawdrier papers had named her back home, she thought with an aching regret for the reputation she had unwittingly cultivated, and which she had left England to escape. And yet it was Kane's harsh opinion of her that had hurt her most, and still did, she realised hopelessly, dropping her grubby bag down onto the pale coverlet of the bed, before sliding back the door to the *en suite*.

The oyster-coloured shower and basin and the blending marble of the counter tops brought a small, appreciative curve to her lips. It seemed a long time since she had enjoyed luxury like this. It was something she had relinquished when she had decided to make a bid for freedom, run from the gossip and the papers, from her father's dictatorship and increasing disapproval, and stand on her own two feet.

There was no evidence of Kane's occupation in here though, and, grateful for a few moments' respite from her profoundly disturbing awareness of him, she ran the taps and splashed water onto her face, wishing, as she watched the water swirl out of the basin, that she could as easily erase her memories of the past.

She had been nine years old when her mother had died after a riding accident, and forever afterwards Ranulph Bouvier hadn't known what to do with his fast-developing, much too adventurous daughter. Her life had become a series of expensive boarding schools and, during the holidays, trips abroad with whatever grudging member of his staff he could pay to accompany her. What she had wanted—needed—was her father's love and affection, but he was always too busy, too preoccupied to give her any time. Instead he had indulged her to the nth degree. Fast cars. Jewellery. Clothes. And, of course, holidays. She had had it all, but unfortunately, Shannon thought sadly, it wasn't enough. She would have forfeited all the trappings of her father's wealth for a loving and harmonious relationship with him—to be able to talk to him about her dreams and aspirations, have her opinions taken seriously—but Ranulph Bouvier wasn't the sort of man who would listen to anyone.

Perhaps it was his refusal to accept that she wanted to do something more worthwhile with her life than simply support a suitable husband, as her mother had, that had set her on that course of single-minded rebellion. The all-night parties. The publicity. The questionable company. At the time it had seemed to fulfil a need for the love and attention that was missing from her life; a need to be noticed. But the fulfilment was superficial and short-lived, like every relationship she tried to form with any of the men who pursued her. And as her disillusionment grew, so did her father's disapproval. He didn't like the way she was behaving: her inability to stick with one boyfriend, the adverse publicity she was courting. Didn't she know she was making a fool of herself? Developing the worst possible kind of reputation? But she couldn't help it if every man she took an interest in just seemed to be after her money, her body, or both.

All except Kane Falconer, that was.

Replacing the towel on its gleaming rail, she moved back into the bedroom. The large bed with its plump pillows beckoned invitingly, and the blind at its porthole was pulled down against the fierce heat of the Spanish sun.

Perhaps she would do as he'd suggested, she thought, and lie down for a while. The problem in town was going to take some time to sort out and it would be ludicrous even considering going home until it was safe.

Subsiding onto the sumptuous bed, she tried not to think about where Kane slept when he was on board. Nevertheless, she couldn't prevent him from intruding unsettlingly on her thoughts, just as he had been doing since she was seventeen.

She had been dangerously affected by the man from the moment she had first set eyes on him, the day she had called into the modern Bouvier office building and seen him sitting there behind her father's desk, as if he belonged there.

He hadn't looked up for a moment, but a moment was all it had taken for the full impact of those compelling good looks and that hard virility to print themselves forever on her consciousness.

Staring down at his groomed dark head, at the breadth of his shoulders beneath the sophisticated cut of his dark jacket, she had started fidgeting, a little irritated that he hadn't noticed her. Everyone noticed her. She had been wearing a black silk suit that day with her hair swept up, and she could still remember how sensuously the low-cut jacket and trousers moved against her body.

He had looked up then, as though it had only just dawned on him that she was there—although she'd known that that wasn't the case, that very little would get past a man like him—and, tall as she was herself in her four-inch heels, as he'd risen to his feet she had felt unusually eclipsed by his dominating height.

'Kane Falconer.' His voice was deep and sexy, and as he reached across the deck her irritation melted under the blaze of his smile. 'The newest assignee to the board.' The board of directors, that was, which gave him top-notch status. The fingers that clasped hers were warm and firm, their contact so overwhelming that she completely forgot her manners and failed to return the courtesy of an introduction, hearing herself stammering uncharacteristically instead, 'W-where's my father?'

'Your...' Clarity dawned in eyes that reminded her of a cool blue alpine lake beneath the thick sable of long lashes. 'So *you're* Jezebel,' he remarked, with his mouth twitching at the corners, repeating the name that one of the newspapers had so detrimentally used to describe her.

Had she been older, perhaps she would have laughed about it, Shannon decided in retrospect. As it was, for all her confidence, she had been too insecure and already hopelessly ensnared by that hard dynamism of his to take such unprovoked criticism from him lightly.

Feigning nonchalance as a protective armour, she had murmured, 'If you say so. Didn't she flout convention and shame herself by wearing red to the ball when every other woman wore white?' She remembered watching a video once of the old Hollywood film. And when the man behind the desk dipped his head in the subtlest acknowledgment, she'd continued, 'Perhaps they should have named me Danielle,' with a forced little laugh. 'For daring to stand alone.'

'*Daniel,*' he corrected, releasing her at last, 'was a man. And he faced lions—which I would have said was far preferable to a gossip-hungry press. And you're just a girl.' He might have thought so, but in that moment when those cool eyes moved over the smooth length of her throat, touched on the swell of her pale breasts beneath the low-cut jacket, she grew up; knew that she had met her match and, with a throbbing recognition, her mate. 'Doesn't it hurt or bother you?' he said. 'What they're printing?'

Of course it did, but let anyone know it and they would have won—torn her to pieces, she thought bitterly. So, with the slightest movement of her shoulder that unintentionally exposed more of her breast to that hard masculine gaze, she answered, 'What? That I'm seen at every wild party from here to John O'Groats and that I change my boyfriends as often as I change my underwear?' She couldn't believe she was quoting such derogatory statements to him, not only because they were totally untrue, but also because she had never in her young life met a man on whom she had so instantly wanted—no, needed—to make a good impression. Nevertheless, she felt herself cringing as she shrugged again and said, 'Why should it?', knowing that she couldn't have sounded less bothered—as he'd put it—if she'd tried.

'It hurts your father.' He rocked back on his heels, surveying her with narrowed eyes and a dark heat that startlingly she recognised as something other than anger; something basic and feral. 'But perhaps that's the intention.'

Even while reeling from the shock of a mutual sexual chemistry, Shannon felt the sting of his remark like a whip across her face. Who did this man think he was? What right did he have to speak to her like this when he didn't even know her? When he didn't know anything about her—or of her unhappy relationship with her father?

'I don't know who you are, or what you're doing here, Mr Falconer. But I don't think my private life—or anyone else's in this family—is any of your concern! Unless you think your duties include trying to take me in hand and dragging me back onto the straight and narrow—in which case I can tell you now, you're wasting your time!'

He was moving some papers on the desk with those long,

well-shaped hands, but glanced up, looking totally unperturbed by her outburst.

'I've no intention of dragging you anywhere, Shannon.' It was the first time he had spoken her name and, despite everything, hearing the way he said it in that deep, rich baritone voice made the hairs stand up on the back of her neck. 'Much as I wouldn't balk at the challenge, I'm rather opposed to seeing my name in the tabloids.'

She walked out of the office that day with her head held high, yet close to tears, having completely forgotten why she had gone there in the first place.

After that she tried to avoid him, but, of course, it was impossible. Having struck a hit with Ranulph Bouvier from the outset, Kane was often invited to the house for dinner. Sometimes she found herself having to speak to him if he rang her father at home—totally unaware of how even his deep, disembodied voice had the power to make her insides melt; her loins burn with a tense and feverish heat. And then, of course, he was at every company function that Ranulph insisted she attend.

'How old are you?' she found the courage to ask him after he had asked her to dance at that last company dinner.

And he replied, 'Too old for you.'

Approaching nineteen, confident of her looks and a sexuality she had sometimes despaired of, she laughed up into his strong, exciting face and, using everything that was feminine in her to try and break through his hard imperviousness towards her, answered sweetly, 'And what makes you think that that simple question suggests I'd want you?'

Her boldness surprised him, but he merely laughed under his breath and pulled her shockingly close.

'Because I'm probably the only man in London who hasn't shown any inclination to bed you,' he returned, his smile blazing, his eyes coolly sardonic. 'And one thing I strongly suspect about you, Shannon, is that your greatest challenges are the things you know you can't have.'

Though she laughed it off, his remark depressed her, assuring her that, when it came to getting Kane Falconer to like her—let alone want her—she was wasting her time. He was too experienced, much too clever for her to outwit, argue with or even try to use her teenage charms on, and in his company she merely suffered one frustrating humiliation after another.

When she started seeing Jason Markham and he asked her to spend the summer with him at his lochside cottage in Scotland she grabbed the chance, as an opportunity to escape not only her father's increasing domination, but also her hopeless feelings for Kane. They were, she decided, blind and stupidly juvenile; outrageously sexual; agonisingly intense.

Her relationship with Jason, on the other hand, provided her with something far less dramatic, along with friendship, of which, at the time, she seemed to be in short supply. Most of the women she tried to befriend since she had blossomed into womanhood seemed to view her only as a sexual rival, and most men as a means of boosting their egos.

Jason seemed interested in her as a person. He listened to her ideas; seemed to share her dreams. And if the relationship was a little less passionate to start with than he had hoped, well, he had no intention of rushing her—he was a patient man, he assured her, content to wait. And that was how she felt—content and comfortable. As one should feel with a person you were considering making a life with, she managed to convince herself. Not so crazy with wanting that you felt you'd burst from the agony of it; not like the mindless, adolescent crush she had harboured for Kane. And if Jason never drove her to those frenzied heights she had dreamed of reaching in Kane Falconer's arms…well, wasn't that for the best? What she felt for Jason was real, not something imagined; real and whole and lasting. Because Jason Markham, up-and-coming racing driver and son of a prominent cabinet minister, was real. Jason was there. Jason was hers.

Which was why, when the story hit the headlines of his wife's suicide attempt following his infidelity, the tabloids had a field day, citing Shannon as the proverbial *femme fatale* with Markham as the hapless victim.

Numb with disbelief—over being lied to—she returned to London to face a barrage of questions she refused to answer, as well as a double dose of her father's temper when she discovered that Kane Falconer had had a disagreement with him that same week and walked out.

She knew Kane had on more than one occasion been head-hunted by the competition; knew he'd found Ranulph difficult to work with. But after the pain of her own betrayal by a man she had convinced herself she was in love with, or at the very least trusted, Kane's defection lanced her to the quick.

Disillusioned, hurting, she was alone at the house when he called that weekend to pick up some personal papers, when the scandal she was at the centre of turned his usual mocking detachment into full-blown anger with her after she pelted him with an angry tirade of abuse.

'You dare to question my behaviour?' His eyes were hard with hostility. 'That's rich coming from an attention-seeking little socialite who'll stop at nothing to get her kicks! And I can think of far worse names, Shannon, but I'll spare you those.' She didn't realise then that he was a friend of Jennifer Markham's family, which must have accounted for why he was so angry. 'I only hope you find what you're looking for—for your sake as well as everybody else's!' he sliced at her as he crossed to the door.

Stung by his opinion, by his leaving, by the frustration of never having had this man on her side, she flung back at him, 'You called me a Jezebel the first time you saw me. Well, if I'm a Jezebel, you're a Judas! Crossing over to the other side!'

It was her hurt anger that had made her say it; and her envy that he was free to walk away, because secretly she admired him for standing up to her father. He wasn't a yes man—not a man her father, or anyone for that matter, could push around.

He'd walked out then, slamming the front door behind him, and she hadn't seen him again until today. Rumour had it that he hadn't joined another company immediately. She even recalled Ranulph saying he'd cut off his nose to spite his face and that he'd live to regret walking out on Bouvier's the way he had. But he hadn't, she thought, if this yacht was anything to go by. He'd obviously got another lucrative post; used those skills and that amazing insight to take him to the top in some other company...

She yawned widely, the occasional gentle motion of the boat relaxing her, making her eyelids heavy...he'd obviously done all right for himself.

The evening sun was streaking gold across the water and, standing on the aft deck, Kane breathed in the cooling air coming off the sea.

Across the wharf the traffic was moving again. He could hear the hum of engines, noticed the first lights coming on in the bars and cafés around the marina, and found himself thinking back to that day, nearly a year ago, when he had answered that distress call from Ranulph Bouvier.

He had found him then, because of circumstances he could so easily have predicted, distraught, driving himself too hard, a near broken man. He had brought it all on himself, Kane knew, but he'd been unable to hold that against the man. Ranulph had needed his help and advice, and Kane had been too worried about him and the company he had once worked for to refuse.

The man was killing himself, he thought. The doctors had told him to take things easy, but it wasn't just the problems of the company that were driving him into the ground, Kane was sure. It was his estrangement from Shannon that was responsible for that.

On the evening breeze he could still hear Ranulph's words as he'd stood with him that first evening on the patio of the Bouvier mansion. *Find my daughter! For pity's sake, find my daughter! Find her and...*

Effectively, he brought the shutters down over the rest of their conversation, and yet that genuine plea from his old employer still tore at his heart.

The man was a tyrant—an oppressor—yet, handled correctly, he was like a tiger with all its teeth pulled out...loud but harmless. And he wanted his daughter back.

Kane inhaled another deeply impatient sigh. So what if he did? It was none of his business. He might have the know-how to turn the fortunes of a company around, but what he knew about human relationships—father and daughter relationships—he could write on a postage stamp. True, he'd made several attempts to find her—and for his own reasons. But it had been a difficult year, and he had had very little time to go chasing missing heiresses, and when he had had the time he had always drawn a blank. Until today...

And now he had found her, he was beginning to wish he hadn't. She didn't look—wasn't—well, and he was immensely concerned over what she might be doing to herself.

If only he could make her see sense. Persuade her to go home before she wound up making herself really ill, he thought, anxiety clenching his jaw from the futility of his wishful thinking. Because how could he expect to do that in just a couple of hours? he asked himself, cursing his schedule, for once impatient with the commitments he had made that left him very little time.

Above the marina, his glance fell on the imposing monument of Columbus; noticed for the first time that the great man was pointing, not westwards towards the Americas he had discovered, but to the east, and the glittering expanse of the Mediterranean Sea. Inside Kane's head, a thought took root, sprouted, expanded and grew.

She'll hate you for this, Falconer, he warned himself, swinging round and crossing the deck with sudden, calculating purpose. And that, he decided wryly, was something he would have to deal with when the time came.

CHAPTER THREE

THE drone of the helicopter was growing louder. The children were laughing and waving, calling to her while the whirr of blades kept drawing nearer, whipping through the heat and the dust. She could just make out the faces of the children now. They weren't laughing any more. They were looking at her in alarm—some were crying, others screaming—while she lashed frantically at the air, and the sound wasn't the buzz of a helicopter any more, but of a whole hatch of attacking insects...

'*No!*' Shannon shot up, heart thudding, face buried in her cupped hands as she gasped for air.

It was all right, she thought, looking around her, trying to steady her breathing. She had just fallen asleep and she was still in the cabin on Kane's boat—a swift survey of the pale lacquered wood and rich furnishings around her confirmed it—and the sound she had heard was the throb of the—

Quickly she sat upright on the big, luxurious bed, frowning, listening. The *engine*? she thought, puzzled.

Feet groping for the mules she had kicked off—goodness knew how long before!—Shannon thrust her toes into them and raced over to peer through the blind.

Through the oval porthole, Barcelona was just a view, and a rapidly diminishing view at that, she realised, aghast.

Without wasting a second, she stumbled back across the cabin, unsteady from the motion, still groggy with sleep.

Kane wasn't at the lower helm, she noticed as she emerged from below and saw the vacant control seats behind the galley, which meant he had to be powering the boat from the upper deck.

He was sitting at the helm as she climbed the steep steps to the flybridge, and was steering the vessel through the open waters, capable hands dealing with the wheel.

He had changed out of his suit into a black T-shirt and jeans and, in spite of everything, Shannon couldn't fail to notice the width and power of his shoulders, how dauntingly masculine he was, as she came across the open deck.

'Where are we going?'

He sent a surprised glance up at her as she moved to stand beside him, her pale features challenging, her hair blowing softly in the wind.

'So you're awake at last,' he observed, returning his attention to the various switches and screens on the instrument panel. 'How are you feeling?'

How could he dare ask that? Impatiently, Shannon glared down at his bent head. The rays of the low sun were picking out the fiery highlights in his hair. 'I said, where are we going?'

He was monitoring something on the panel, didn't even look up as he said, 'You might have been killing time back there, Shannon, but I wasn't. I've got a schedule to meet.'

'A sched— What schedule?' she demanded anxiously. They were cruising at a rate of knots, each powerful slicing of the waves carrying them further and further into the open sea. 'Where the hell do you think you're taking me?' she demanded again.

He was handling the craft with the skill of a master, she realised as she waited for his answer, looking behind at the sun streaking fire across their foaming wake.

'I have to deliver this thing to Cannes before the end of the week and I've already lost valuable time,' he told her phlegmatically, 'so I'm afraid you're going to have to stick with me until delivery.'

'Cannes. *Cannes!*' she repeated, horrified. She couldn't believe he was saying this. He had to be joking surely? 'That's France!'

His mouth moved in mock appreciation as he kept his course, making progress seaward, still following the coast. 'Ten out of ten for geography, Shannon. It's good to know you learnt something at those fancy schools you attended.'

'You arrogant louse!' With a swish of her hair, angrily she glared at the diminishing coastline, then Kane's hard countenance again. 'Turn this thing around this minute!' And when he simply ignored her, sitting there with that determined thrust to his jaw: 'I said turn it around!' she ordered.

'I'm sorry, Shannon. I can't do that,' he said calmly. 'As I told you, I'm already behind schedule. I'm down a crew member from my outbound journey and you've already admitted you weren't doing anything particular back there.'

'You abduct me...and you've got the audacity to ask me to crew for you?' It came out as a squeak.

'You said you were looking for excitement.'

'I said—' Had she said that?

'And I know you've done it for your father.'

Yes, in the past. He had even come out on the yacht with them once or twice, she remembered, recalling how excited—how gauche—she had felt in his company. But that was different...

'So you're kidnapping me to do it?' Suddenly fear was the overriding emotion, fear and a deepening anger over the fact that he had tricked her onto the vessel in the first place. 'If you don't turn this thing around, so help me, I'll swim back!'

'Don't be ridiculous!'

'Just watch me!' Already she was stumbling away, unaware of Kane reducing their speed, only of knocking her hip on the hard casing that housed a fridge and barbecue, in her crazy bid to carry out her threat.

'Don't be such a fool!' As she made it to the steps, he was

just that bit too quick for her and she let out a small cry when his arm came round her middle like an iron bar.

'Let me go!' She twisted round in his grasp, pummelling at the hard wall of his chest. 'Let me go, you big bully!'

'For heaven's sake, Shannon! Calm down! Do you really think I would have chosen to bring you with me? I'd already lost valuable time through my meeting starting late this afternoon, but you were sleeping far too peacefully for me to disturb. You had a pretty hard smack on the head—and even without that, you weren't in any fit state for me to leave back there!'

Head swimming, feeling weak—but from his nearness—forcibly, she pulled out of his grasp. 'Oh, so now you're doing it for my benefit!'

'Ultimately, I hope so.'

The evening sun was dazzling, making her squint as she tilted her head to look challengingly up at him. 'What's that supposed to mean?'

'It means that I think you could do with a few days' looking-after. And if I can persuade you to see what you're doing to yourself—what you're throwing away by not facing facts and going home in the process—so much the better!'

Anger turned her eyes almost to sapphire. 'What do you mean? Face facts? What facts?'

'A company that will very probably be yours one day—whether you like it or not. A father who isn't getting any younger.'

Anxiety was suddenly replacing the hot emotion staining her cheeks, corrugating her otherwise smooth forehead. 'You said you hadn't seen him.'

'No, I didn't.'

Hadn't he? She couldn't remember all of what he had said back there in Las Ramblas.

'What, then? He's all right, isn't he?' The question was a worried whisper.

'Is that actual concern I see, Shannon?'

'What do you think?' she snapped, recognising scepticism in that hard face. Ranulph Bouvier might not have shown himself to be a loving and affectionate parent, but he *was* her father.

'What I think is that it's time you stepped off the merry-go-round of socialising and living it up with your fancy friends and start to consider that your father might possibly need you. Consider that in some things he might also be right instead of opposing and rebelling against everything he stands for just for the sheer hell of it!'

'For the sheer hell of it?' Was that what he thought? 'Why?' she contested angrily. 'If I happen to disagree with a lot of what he believes in? I might be a lot of things, but I'm not a hypocrite, Kane. And I don't recall you always being so deferential to my father. In fact, you were very much against him when you walked out and left him in the lurch!'

His mouth took on a grim cast. Perhaps he didn't like being reminded, she thought suddenly, wondering also if he remembered how bitterly they had faced each other that last time he had called at the house.

'If anyone left him in the lurch it was his dearly beloved and very wayward daughter! And only after she'd managed to drag the Bouvier name through the mud!'

'That's not true!' she defended, her flesh tautening over her high, gaunt cheeks as she remembered. She had been slated—and unjustly—by a scandal-raking Press; made a scapegoat and a victim by people who had more power than she had and who, after putting her through the wringer, had effectively hung her out to dry. But being misunderstood and blamed by a father who was too busy and uninterested even to notice what was happening to his only child was worse than anything else. 'And I left because he refused to acknowledge that I had views and opinions—just as you did!'

'With one difference,' Kane uttered succinctly.

'Oh?'

'He didn't raise me.'

She turned around with her shoulders hunched, her arms wrapped protectively around her, staring unseeingly at the diminutive buildings of the Spanish mainland in the distance, dark silhouettes against the vivid red ball of the setting sun.

She couldn't go back to the oppression—to being dictated to. Nor could she stand everyone believing the worst about her when her only crime was being taken in by a man she had thought was—to all intents and purposes—free to love her. The fact that he'd ranked highly in a couple of world-class races and had a prominent politician father only served to make the supposed affair front-page news when his still very resident wife had taken that overdose and lost her unborn baby because of it. Perhaps, Shannon thought now, it would have been better if she had divulged her side of the story, but she had remained silent when those reporters had hounded her, preferring to be thought an adulteress rather than a fool. Afterwards Ranulph Bouvier had tried to tighten his control of her, tried to deprive her of her independence and her freedom, until his authority had stifled her. Eventually, only weeks after Kane had left the firm, she had fled London for good.

'Did my father ask you to find me?' Suspicion narrowed her eyes as she turned back to Kane. 'Try to bring me home?' And when he didn't answer, his mouth still set in that inexorable cast, 'So that's it!' she breathed, letting her arms fall in clarification, her pose no longer defensive, but all-attacking now. 'He's got you back working for him again, hasn't he?' she accused, certain of it, her lips tightening mutinously when she noticed that almost indiscernible shrug of his shoulder. 'This is my father's boat, isn't it? It isn't yours at all. And I thought you'd done better for yourself!' She couldn't contain the derisory little laugh that trembled through those last words, her laughter masking the pain she had nursed for what seemed like centuries from his cruel opinion of her; the frustration of never being able to tell him that he was wrong; that nothing was as it seemed. 'So the Bouvier name isn't *that* muddied for you after all!' she continued to taunt him. 'Or was the deal being offered so much more attractive to you this time?'

Almost inaudibly, she heard him catch his breath. 'You think that's all it boils down to, don't you?' he said scathingly. 'Money?' With that he was striding away from her, back to the helm.

'Doesn't it?' Shannon, following, threw at his broad back. In her experience, it had ranked very highly on most people's list of priorities, in the men she had met, in the obvious hangers-on, in the long line of superficial, so-called 'friends'. 'What's he offered you? A nice fat bonus if you bring me back?' She watched him take up his position behind the wheel again and increase the vessel's speed with a swift, controlling ease. 'Whatever he's paying you, I'll double it,' she suggested desperately through the sudden, ominous throbbing of the powerful engine.

'Out of your allowance?' From that half-cocked eyebrow, as the boat surged forward, he looked remarkably sceptical.

Perhaps he thought she couldn't afford him, she considered, wondering how much he knew.

'I have assets!' she assured him, clutching the cool steel of a handrail, having to raise her voice above the upsurge of the water, the rush of the stiff and freshening wind. There was the jewellery she hadn't wanted. The paintings she had left back in England. Not Monets or Constables, it was true, but certainly worth a lot of money by anyone's standards. And there was her Porsche...

'So I see.'

'Not that!' she berated, when she saw the way his eyes were roving over the slender lines of her body with mocking sensuality, causing her breathing to quicken, her cheeks to flame from the realisation that he had deliberately misinterpreted what she had meant.

'I'm relieved to hear it,' he called back over the increasing turbulence of the water, 'for both our sakes. Much as I find you tempting, it's not my policy to get involved with news-courting little socialites, so your honour's quite safe, if that's what you're worried about.' And then, before she could retaliate, stung as she was by his remarks, he was adding, 'And what makes you think your father's offered me anything?'

'Because I know my father.' Deftly she watched him flick a switch, saw a jumble of data appear on one of the screens. 'And I know now that, like most people, you can be bought if the price is right.'

'Well, Shannon,' he said without looking at her, 'I'm afraid taking you back there is going to cost me far more than you can afford.' Then with a pointed glance at her small breasts and the logo stamped blatantly across them, 'so I'm afraid,' he intoned firmly, 'the bulls are going to have to manage without your gallant support for a while.'

'You...' The little invective she uttered was barely audible above the boat's powerful slicing through the waves. 'And I used to think you were a cut above the rest.'

For a moment as his eyes met hers she saw in his a silent query; a studied contemplation as though she had surprised him with that reckless little confession. Swiftly, though, he was turning away, giving all his attention to the task of steering and navigation. 'I'm sorry to disappoint you,' he said.

Lips tightening, Shannon swung away from him, down the steps and through the doors into the saloon, where she flopped wearily onto one of the pale leather settees. He'd said he was sorry to disappoint her. Well, she was sorry too, she thought.

She had always admired and envied him: his candidness; his refusal to be anything but his own man. Now she was profoundly disappointed to discover that, when it came down to it, he was just the same as everybody else.

And why? she asked herself bitterly. Surely these feelings he still aroused were only the leftovers of a fierce and painful adolescent crush? And even if she was still affected by that hard, masculine, bred-in-the-bone confidence and by his intensely powerful sexuality, it was only that, just sexual, after all.

Which was just as well, she decided with a sudden clenching of her teeth, because he had certainly made it clear—and with no beating about the bush—that he wasn't interested in her! As far as he was concerned, she was just a spoilt rich bitch whom he was being paid to return to where he thought she belonged, without knowing anything about her, what made her tick, her values, her hopes, her dreams.

Well, carry on, Kane Falconer! she thought, flicking angrily through a glossy magazine she had plucked from the floor-mounted coffee table before tossing it back down again. You don't know anything about me—nor are you going to! she determined wretchedly, retreating behind the wall of self-protection she had built around herself. If you want to think the worst about me, then carry on!

Having glanced back over his shoulder when Shannon had stormed off, Kane hadn't failed to notice that deflated look about her.

She had said she'd thought him a cut above the rest, which surprised him immensely, but he was also surprised to discover how much it pleased him too. He had always thought her opinion of him low to say the least, and now, because of the way she had sounded when she had—unintentionally, he felt—dispelled him of that notion, suddenly he felt like a first-rate heel. He'd condemned her, not because everybody else did. It had never been in his nature to listen to mere gossip—follow the common trend—but because, like everyone else with a gram of common sense, he could see the road she was going down, and he couldn't deny that that crazy lifestyle of hers invited criticism. But even the most condemned of men—or women, he amended wryly—deserved a hearing, and he hadn't even allowed her that. Perhaps he should have left her back there, instead of trying to get her to see things his way when she was so hell-bent on refusing to. But if he had, and then something happened to her...

He shook off the thought, wishing he didn't feel so inextricably involved.

She had been right, when she had accused him of being seduced back to Bouvier's by an attractive deal, although it wouldn't have been in his interests—and much less the company's—to refuse. But if she really knew the 'deal' Ranulph had initially offered him for bringing her home—a deal he himself had had no compunction about turning down flat— she would probably have jumped over the side without a backward glance.

Checking the compass, estimating the distance from his intended mooring, he wondered if she had believed him when he had admitted to being worried about her; wondered whether, in using her health and safety as the only reason for keeping her with him, he was being entirely honest with himself.

Because the whole truth was that, ever since the first day he had seen her when she had breezed into her father's office nearly five years ago, she had stirred in him every masculine instinct it was possible to stir. Concern. Anger. Protectiveness. As well as downright lust! And that was it, he thought, despairing at himself, because, young as she had been then— and angry—as she had been that last time when she had stood there calling him a Judas, she had had the power to arouse him, and still arouse him, like no other girl or woman he had ever met.

With a tense clamping of his jaw, fingers tightening around the wheel, he steered the powerful vessel through the gathering dusk. How the hell he was going to keep his mind on getting this thing to Cannes with her on board was anybody's guess when he wanted to undress her every time he looked at her. Even in that urchin outfit he found himself wanting to peel her clothes off her, and he had only made that ridiculously outmoded statement about her honour to warn himself to watch his own step. Even thinking about her lying on that big bed—as she'd been earlier when he had gone below with some tea and found her sleeping, her blonde hair splashed across the pillow—filled his mind with thoughts that were anything but honourable. Just as in the past, even while he'd been bitterly disappointed and angry with her—with himself—after that scandalous affair, for still wanting her, he found himself envying every man whose bed she might have shared, wanting to be the one whose name that soft voice whispered, for whom those blue eyes grew heavy with desire; to hear her moan in acquiescence as he kissed the pale satin of her body and feel his own body harden—as it was doing now—from the unbelievable ecstasy of pleasuring her...

'What happened to your last passenger?'

'What?' He swung round so fast that he almost sent a mug beside the control panel flying.

'Your last passenger. The one who helped you crew? What happened to them?' Shannon repeated.

'Nothing *happened* to them.' He sounded tense—impatient, she noted, her eyes drawn reluctantly to those strong, tanned hands steadying a mug; hands, she realised through that familiar unwelcome tension, that were experienced in handling more than just an ocean-cruiser... 'She got off in Barcelona.'

She?

That casually delivered piece of information shook Shannon for a moment, her lack of immediate response bringing Kane's gaze sliding over her in a way that made her skin tingle. But telling herself that it was no business of hers whom he had on board, trenchantly she said, 'Why? Did she get fed up with your bullying?'

'No.'

The certainty in his voice sent a shaft of emotion through her that she didn't wish to question.

'What was she?' she tossed back, fighting it. 'Some sort of masochist?'

She glimpsed amusement playing around his mouth before he turned back to the controls.

Had she slept with him? Shannon wondered, stomach muscles tightening just from looking at those powerful forearms. Shared endless hours of fun with him in the private master suite, the stairs to which she had glimpsed just inside the saloon? Well, of course she had! she thought with a swift surge of unwarranted resentment that wasn't solely to do with being on board against her will. Now she understood why he had been so quick to let her know that he wasn't interested in *her*.

'Are you hungry?' He had eased back the throttle, and was cruising now at a far more leisurely pace.

Staring out at their lights reflected on the darkening sea, hands stuck into the back pockets of her trousers, Shannon said mutinously, 'Not so much that I'd take anything from you.'

He didn't take his own eyes off their course. 'Suit yourself,' he said phlegmatically. 'It's a long way to Cannes.'

Tramping below, Shannon paced the luxurious saloon, clasping her bent arm as she nibbled on a nail. What was she supposed to do? she wondered, exasperated. She couldn't just sit here and complain while he shipped her all the way to the French Riviera. And from that unwavering determination she had met when she had asked him to take her back, there was no way she was going to be able to persuade him to.

Deciding that she had to eat while she thought up some other plan, she traipsed up the carpeted steps to the galley.

He must have switched on the lights earlier because now

there was a soft glow illuminating the steel fittings of the taps and the marble counters.

She started opening cupboards and banging them closed again, making a statement in defiance of his thinking that she was doing anything other than unwillingly. Eventually, finding several convenience meals in need of heating in the refrigerator, she took one out and stuck it in the microwave oven, pressing several of the buttons to a series of agitated bleeps before the unfamiliar appliance suddenly hummed into life.

Leaving the meal heating, she went back out on deck, almost colliding with Kane as he came leaping down the steps from the flybridge.

Darkness had well and truly fallen now, the sinking sun replaced by a huge full moon that threw a bright silver path across the waves.

'Perhaps it has slipped your mind…' she broke off, breathless, finding him too big, too imposing in the shadowy intimacy of the covered aft deck '…but what exactly am I supposed to do for clothes?'

With his face in shadow, she could only sense the amusement that tilted the corners of his mouth as he indicated for her to go back inside and followed her in.

'I'm sure there is something in one of the wardrobes in your cabin that might fit you,' he drawled, switching on the saloon lights, before disappearing down the stairs, presumably to check something in the engine room.

Which meant what? Shannon wondered curiously, as it dawned. That his last, adoring passenger had begun the trip in her own berth and then very accommodatingly moved into his?

'If you think I'm wearing one of your girlfriends' cast-offs, you've got another thing coming!' she breathed, affronted, as he came back up again, wondering how serious his relationship might be with the woman for her to have left her belongings on board. As though she expected to be back…

'Well, you've got to get out of those some time, and if you don't mind the alternative…' in spite of what he had said about not being interested in her, his eyes ran over her slender figure as though he was imagining her naked '…I'm sure I don't.'

Shannon felt colour creeping up her throat into her cheeks, and was relieved when a sudden cheesy aroma made him sniff the air and say, 'Mmm, something smells good.'

'That's my supper,' Shannon found great pleasure in responding. 'If you think I'm cooking for you after you've had the gall to trick me on here—bring me on this trip against my will—then you're going to be sorely disappointed!'

'A spirited little thing, aren't you? I always thought so, but until today I hadn't realised just how much.'

'And what have you been told to do on this trip? Break me in?'

'Now, that would make for an interesting voyage.' Shannon tensed as he reached out and, having caught a strand of golden hair, was winding it insolently around his index finger, tugging gently so that it was all that she could do not to sway towards him, to stand her ground. That musky scent of his teased her nostrils and Shannon's breathing quickened, fear of her own responses putting a wary challenge in her eyes. 'Don't worry,' he said, disconcertingly aware. 'Taming feisty, undisciplined females isn't altogether my idea of fun, even if I have always believed that a good spanking in the beginning might not have done you any harm.'

She didn't realise that she had struck him until she felt her hand smarting. Released now, she stared, horrified, at his reddening cheek.

'I'll have you know I'm nearly twenty-two and the way I conduct my life has nothing, absolutely nothing, to do with you,' she breathed in a trembling whisper when she was able to speak again. 'Or with anybody else.'

He put up his hands, palms outwards, as though calling for a truce. His jaw was clenched and his chest was rising and falling as though he had been exercising hard.

'OK. Maybe I deserved that,' he accepted, sounding breathless. 'However, let's get one thing clear. It wasn't my intention to trick you to come aboard—nor did I. This was only my idea of a safe haven until the problems back there...' this with an upward jerk of his chin '...quietened down. I wouldn't have chosen to lumber myself with a fiery wildcat on this trip if circumstances hadn't dictated otherwise.'

'Like my health?' she threw after him, because he had already stepped outside and was heading for the flybridge steps again.

'You're damn right, like your health!' he tossed back at her when he saw her following him up.

'How very magnanimous!' She couldn't help the little jibe, something inside her stupidly aching to hear him say one kind word.

'Not entirely. I already told you, I'm behind schedule,' he stressed, taking up his position again at the wheel. 'I promised I'd be in Cannes with this thing by Thursday—and there I intend to be. If I haven't managed to persuade you to see sense by then—and *if* I think you're well enough, then I'll see you get back to Barcelona.'

'Bravo!' The moonlight streaked silver across her hair as she stood there beside him with her hands planted firmly on her hips. 'And that makes kidnapping me all right?'

'Our first port of call's St Tropez,' he went on, the impervious skipper once more, back in control. 'If you want clothes I'm sure the shops there can come up with something to suit even your exclusive tastes.'

Another dig, she realised, at the girl he thought she was, the girl he thought he knew. Not the real Shannon Bouvier—

the one with feelings, with hopes and dreams. Well, she'd show him!

'Please don't concern yourself about my tastes or my health, Mr Kane High and Mighty Falconer, because I've got news for you! The instant we reach dry land, I'm not hanging around for your permission. I'm catching the first plane back!'

Which were idle words, she thought self-mockingly, because she didn't have the money for a bus, let alone an airline ticket! Being unwell and unable to work for weeks had taken quite a slice out of her savings, and what was left had had to be used to clear the debts she had unknowingly and unintentionally incurred. Pride wouldn't let her tell Kane that, however; let him know what a sorry state she was in financially; risk Ranulph Bouvier finding out that he had been right; that she couldn't manage on her own.

'That's your prerogative,' Kane said in response to what she had said about flying back at the first opportunity, 'but if you do, you're not much of a daughter.'

She was walking away, but his words brought her up short. Because of course, that was what he was holding her with primarily. Guilt. He would use it—and effectively—to achieve his own ends. His own monetary reward, she thought bitterly.

'Your father's worried about you,' he enlarged then, as though reading her thoughts. 'Worried you're not looking after yourself, and though I'm inclined to agree on the whole…' significantly he massaged the area just below his cheek '…I'd say in some ways you can pretty much take care of yourself.'

'My father thinks no woman's capable of doing anything if there isn't some man running her life,' she said, her tone reproaching, resentful.

'And you're out to prove him wrong?'

'What's wrong with that?'

'Nothing. Only there's a right way and a—' He broke off

as what sounded like an explosion seemed to come from the direction of the galley.

'What the—?'

'Oh, no!'

They had spoken in unison, and now Shannon was racing back to the lasagne she had inadvertently forgotten. The glass door of the microwave was splattered with a gungy mess, she noticed, despairing as she came up into the galley.

'Looks like your supper's had other ideas,' Kane drawled from behind, hurriedly reaching round to switch off the appliance before she could. Deftly he flicked the button to release the door.

Heat and steam belched out with the smell of what had promised to be a very tasty meal. Now tomato sauce and pieces of detonated pasta clung with a glue-like substance to the roof and walls of the oven.

'Perhaps you'd better let me do the cooking in future,' he advised drily, using a cloth to remove the steaming mess that was left of the plastic tray. 'I forgot. It isn't something you were born to, is it?' His tone was softly mocking, making her hackles rise as he dumped the remains of her meal to cool in the sink.

'Not with servants. Hardly!' she sneered, provoked by his cruel opinion of her privileged upbringing. If you could call being abandoned in boarding schools and exclusive hotels while still mourning the loss of your mother privileged! she thought grievously. 'And the type of accommodation I'm used to doesn't call for this kind of self-catering either!'

Nor had there been running water, let alone a bath, or even a roof over her head sometimes. Unless you counted the tarpaulin of a filthy, twenty-year-old truck, she thought heatedly. But she wasn't going to tell Kane that either.

CHAPTER FOUR

SHE was starving, Shannon realised, tossing down the paper-back book—a modern mystery novel—she had found on top of the vanity unit, and slipping off the bed, wondering if Kane had finally managed to clean up the mess she had made of his oven. A short time ago she had heard him anchoring for the night, and now all she could feel was the occasional gentle motion as the boat bobbed and swayed on the calm waters.

She had come down here earlier to get out of his way, deciding that leaving him to do the clearing up served him right for kidnapping her in the first place. Now she wished she had brought a snack down with her after she had declined his offer—and not very graciously—to cook something for her.

'I don't want anything from you,' she had repeated point-edly. 'I'll have something cold.' She had seen some cheeses in the dairy compartment of the fridge and a French stick on one of the counters. 'And I'll have it in my cabin—on my own!'

He'd shrugged and said again, 'Suit yourself,' as though it made very little difference to him.

Now, rummaging through the wardrobe, she found very little in the way of feminine clothing. Besides a beach tunic and a couple of pairs of cropped leggings, there wasn't much else, and definitely no sign of any nightwear.

Probably his lady friend hadn't felt the need of any, Shannon thought crabbily. But what woman would? The taunting little thought sprang into her mind to goad her. With a man like Kane as a bed partner?

Deciding that the beach tunic, at least, might come in

handy, she brushed her hair vigorously without even bothering to look in the mirror, and padded back up to the galley.

Kane was standing at the stove, cooking his own meal and pouring cream over something sizzling and delicious-smelling in a pan. She felt him glance her way as she came up, but she ignored him, moving past him down through the saloon and out into the cool air on deck.

Here, under the canopy at the back of the boat, a table was laid for two, a candle flickering at its centre. So he was expecting her to eat with him, was he? Share his table—and that bottle of white wine she could see sitting in its cooler beside the bread basket—as he had shared it with some other and more willing passenger before her?

With lips tightening in rebellion, Shannon moved around the table, stopping at the top of the steps leading down to the dinghy and the swim platform—the steps, she realised with a strange little shiver, that Kane had used earlier to carry her on.

They were anchored in a moonlit cove. The lights from some coastal buildings twinkled above the shoreline, and away to the east lay the dense darkness of night-shrouded hills. The moon was higher now, laying a pale wash over a large area of the water, and a pleasingly cooling breeze came off the coast, refreshing her, clearing her head.

Where were they now? she wondered. The Spanish-French border? She wasn't sure, and she certainly didn't intend asking Kane.

The smell of cooking drifting out from the galley had her inhaling deeply. Was that Pernod he was using? She couldn't bear it! She was ravenous and he was doing it deliberately— making her mouth water like this, her stomach grumble its craving for the food she had denied it.

About to go back inside just as he was coming out, she turned swiftly away and, with her arms folded, stood with her back to him, looking out to sea as he set the two plates he had been carrying down on the table.

'Come and eat.'

'No.'

He didn't try to persuade her. With increasing annoyance she heard his relaxed, economic movements behind her. The squeak of the upholstered bench that would probably double as a stowage locker. The ring of cutlery on china. The sound of a glass being filled. And all the time that delicious aroma kept teasing her nostrils.

There was a moment's silence when she assumed he tasted the wine. It would be cool and thirst-quenching, she thought, imagining it sliding down her own throat, hearing him swallow with lip-smacking appreciation. 'Mmm. That's good.'

She turned round, glared at him. He was tucking into his meal. She could see the steam rising from his plate as he cut into what she guessed was temptingly prepared scallops. She could taste the flavours, the seasoned oil he had used to cook them. Her pride told her to go inside. Leave him to his smug supper. Her stomach begged her to have mercy.

Her stomach won.

Too humbled to look at him, she sat down on one of the vacant chairs on the opposite side of the table and, reaching for her knife and fork, tore into a scallop. It was soft and succulent, its white flesh seared brown in places from the heated oil, and it melted in her mouth like manna, ripe with Pernod and fennel and cream. She closed her eyes, savouring the heaven of his cooking.

'Isn't it *just*?' he appreciated as though it were something he had invited her to try and which she had willing agreed to—not something snatched begrudgingly from his table. But he made no other comment, for which she was thankful. He had probably already assessed that, had he done so, she would have taken off like a startled doe.

'This is particularly good.' About to pour her some wine,

he stopped, bottle suspended in mid-air. 'I'm sorry. I forgot. You're taking medication, aren't you?'

'Half a glass won't hurt.'

There was a complacent curve to his lips, she noted through the canopy's soft lighting, which could have been because of the way she had thrown herself wholeheartedly into the meal. She strongly suspected, though, that it was from that split-second's sizzling contact between them when, in trying to stop him depriving her of the wine, reaching for the bottle, she had accidentally caught at his hard wrist instead.

'So why the antibiotics?' he enquired when he had poured her wine, replaced the bottle in its cooler. 'What's the story behind the intestinal problem?' He picked up his fork, took another mouthful of his supper. 'Or shouldn't I ask?'

'You can ask,' Shannon responded succinctly, still tingling from the contact, and, after a moment, 'I was away. I got sick. I came home.'

She wasn't prepared to tell him how she had contracted it—or in what capacity. That part of her life was personal, and she didn't feel inclined to share it with someone who was ready to accept payment for taking her home against her will, never mind how good his cooking!

He didn't press the subject. Glass in hand, relaxing back against the upholstered seat, he was studying the soft symmetry of her face and the pale sheen of her hair, bathed silver by the moonlight streaming through the open sunroof of the canopy.

'So how did an archetypal English rose like you manage to wind up with a name like Bouvier?'

His cool regard made her pulses leap, so that she despaired with herself for the way he affected her. She didn't want to be sitting there, making small talk with him, pretending everything was all right, when it wasn't, so she returned rather snappily, 'I thought you and my father were as thick as thieves. Why don't you ask him?'

He sat forward then, those strong masculine features, touched by the night's shadows, taking on a harder edge above the dancing light of the candle. 'I'm asking you.'

His words were tinged with just the right blend of persuasion and authority, a lethal mixture that no woman in her right mind, Shannon decided hopelessly, could fail to respond to.

'I had a French grandfather,' she was telling him before she could stop herself, realising she was no exception.

'What did that mean? A lot of childhood holidays spent in France?'

'A lot of holidays.' *Holidays everywhere.* 'But not particularly in France. Nor with my grandfather.' *Only with anyone in Ranulph's employ who could be persuaded and paid to accompany her.* 'I never knew him. He died before I was born.'

'I'm sorry.'

'Don't be.' She gave a little shrug, breaking off some of the bread-stick she had taken from the basket. 'What you never have, you never miss.'

'Don't you?' She saw him frown. Had he picked up on that betraying little edge to her voice? 'I never knew a grandfather either,' he went on, 'but I can't help feeling somehow deprived by that. And I haven't settled down yet, had kids, but if I never did—particularly where the kids are concerned—I'd feel as though I'd missed out on a great deal.'

His admission surprised her. She had never imagined him to be the family type.

'Children can be a nuisance,' she said quickly, dipping her bread into the delicious sauce around her plate. 'Just ask my father.' And before she could prevent it slipping out, 'Oh, I forgot—you've already done that, haven't you?' she was adding cynically.

The gentle wash of the sea filled the sudden, momentary silence.

'Do you think,' he said, 'that I invest every moment of the valuable time I spend with Ranulph discussing you?'

Didn't he?

Of course not, Shannon thought, realising she had almost wanted to believe he did. But she was far too unimportant to be any more than a passing thought to a man like Kane.

'Of course not,' she uttered aloud. 'Time costs money. And that little word "invest"—' how easily he had used it! '—assures me of just how much it means to you.'

If she had been baiting him, then he didn't rise to it. Calmly, he refilled his glass, offered to top up hers.

She shook her head.

'So are you saying that any children of yours are going to be a thorough nuisance?'

'Definitely not!' Her reply was sharp and decisive. 'I'm going to make them feel wanted! I'm going to...' She broke off, suddenly realising she was in danger of giving too much away.

'Go on.'

She had been going to say that she would give them all the time, love and affection that had been missing from her own life. Instead she substituted, 'Give them everything I never had.'

His features were half in shadow as he looked at her askance. 'Some people might say that isn't very much.'

Well, they would, wouldn't they? she thought bitterly, and with a dismissive little shake of her head uttered, 'You wouldn't understand.'

He put down his knife and fork, sitting forward with his elbows on the table, that strong chin resting on his long, linked hands. 'Try me,' he invited silkily.

She picked up her glass. 'How long have you got?'

'All night if you want it.' She might have imagined the undertone of sensuality behind that remark. Even so, it caught her off-guard, loosening her tongue like pure spirit.

So she told him about her childhood, about losing the mother she'd adored—who had been so much younger than Ranulph—and then her grandmother within six months of each other, about the schools and the childminders, her tone tinged with a cynicism that stopped short of making it an amiable and willing communication, while he pumped, prompted, probed…and listened intently.

She remembered the nights as an eighteen-year-old when she had lain awake in bed and imagined herself talking to him like this, having his undivided attention. Imagined…

Mortified, she realised the way her thoughts were going and her voice was shaking as she asked, 'What about you?'

'What about me?'

'Do you have a background—besides a lack of grandfathers? Any skeletons in your closet? Or were you always Mr Perfect?'

A masculine eyebrow lifted at the jibe, but he chose to ignore it. 'I'm sorry to disappoint you,' he said lightly then, 'but no—no skeletons. I had an average, middle-class upbringing. The usual schooling. University. As for the rest…' His mouth tugged down on one side. 'Are you really interested?' he asked.

'No,' she said quickly, too quickly, although she was, she realised, deep down. Immensely so. She wanted to know everything about him. What he'd been doing since leaving Bouvier's. His hobbies. What the woman whom he had brought here voluntarily—as his equal, as his bed partner—was like. 'No,' she said again, 'but since we've got nothing else to do…'

It was an attempt not to sound as though she was hanging on his every word, and was paid for when he enquired mockingly, 'What else would you rather we were doing, Shannon?'

Their eyes met and held and her throat went dry. Dear heaven! Why did he ask these questions in that deep, sexy voice of his as if she were his woman—as if she were some-one he wanted to be with, when...

She brought up her thoughts quickly. When what? When he'd already made it quite clear that he had no more interest in her than he had when she was seventeen? When she had had every man she met from sixteen to sixty falling over himself to get to know her, lure her into bed—and he hadn't. *Why hadn't he?*

'I want to go to bed.' She got up quickly, accidentally knocking the table with her knee so that the glasses toppled precariously.

Swiftly, though without any of her awkwardness, he was on his feet too. 'I think we should both go to bed,' he stated huskily.

Shannon swallowed, caught in the dangerous snare of his dark sexuality. The air between them was electrified. His gaze on her parted lips burned as though it were his mouth that touched them, touched the moon-washed column of her throat and her responding breasts beneath her clinging top; as though it weren't just the cool steel of his eyes. He hadn't meant that. Not in the way it had sounded, she thought giddily. It was only because of this lethal attraction to him that she had even dared to interpret it in any other way...

'No, not together, Shannon,' he breathed, as though he had read her mind, that cool smile on his lips mortifyingly aware. 'I'm quite sure most men would give their eye teeth to lose themselves to those alluring charms of yours before being cast away like yesterday's newspaper, but I'm not one of them. How do they survive it, I wonder?'

'They don't.' It was a bitter little cry, torn from the very heart of her. 'I wreck their lives, remember?' Just who did he think he was, goading her with his moral rectitude? 'And from the way you keep telling me how immune you are, I'm be-ginning to wonder, Kane Falconer!' Then, before she swung away from him, verbally she lashed out with one last desperate stab at that inexorable pride, 'The gentleman doth protest too much, methinks!'

She was in tears before she had even reached her cabin.

Watching her go, Kane could have kicked himself.

You really loused that up, Falconer, he cursed to himself. Why the devil he had had to provoke her like that, he didn't know. Or perhaps he did, and just didn't want to admit it, he thought with a self-deprecating grimace. It was simply that he wanted this girl; wanted her in his bed—in his life; wanted to sate himself with the taste and touch and scent of her, and yet contrarily he didn't believe that any man could be her lover and remain unscathed.

He remembered that tabloid photograph of Jason Markham pictured with his adoring wife; remembered the words the man had used to vindicate his affair with Shannon Bouvier.

I was bewitched!

And how effectively she had twisted the knife in his own, easily gouged pride when she had mocked his constant need to deny how much she affected him. Because, of course, he was in just as much danger of being bewitched, he warned himself, which was why he had to keep denying it, refuse to allow this girl—no matter how tempting she was—to bring him to his knees.

In spite of everything, though, she was still very young. Too young to feel the degree of bitterness she was harbouring. And he suspected it wasn't just a betraying lover, or the Press, that was responsible for it. She wasn't very forthcoming about her life as a whole, but from what she had told him—and that rather reluctantly—it sounded as though she had had it tough where relationships were concerned and he had already guessed, without being told, that Ranulph Bouvier wasn't the world's most understanding or affectionate parent.

His daughter didn't trust anyone, but particularly men, and

there was no way that he, Kane Falconer, was going to do anything to add to that.

Shannon wasn't sure what had disturbed her, but the light seeping in through the shallow blind suggested that it was barely dawn.

A sudden splash outside, followed by several more, had her slipping, naked, out of bed, bringing her over to the starboard-side window.

Her dreams had been filled with strange and curious sounds. But perhaps they weren't all in her dreams, she realised, shielding her eyes, unable to make out anything from the brilliance of the sun's rays on the water.

All seemed quiet on board, which had to mean that Kane was still asleep in his cabin, she thought, expecting nothing else. Grabbing one of the oyster-coloured towels from the bathroom and fastening it, sarong-style, above her breasts, she made her way silently but swiftly up onto the aft deck.

Despite the early hour, the day was already warming up, bathing her throat and shoulders with its gentle heat as she stepped out from under the canopy and the scene of last night's tense little supper.

The rocky cove where they were anchored had a shingle beach. Easily within swimming distance, she calculated. There was a way up through the scrub too, a dangerous, though not impossible path, she noted, shielding her eyes again before looking seawards.

The sunrise was laying a gold sheen across the water, so brilliant it was almost painful to observe. There was scarcely a ripple, other than a gentle lapping sound against the hull. It was so calm and still it was almost impossible to believe she had heard what she thought she had heard from the cabin. Then something broke the surface of the water about ten metres out, a swift grey shape leaping up out of the depths, followed by another, then another.

Gasping with wonder, laughing her surprise, Shannon could only stand and watch as the sleek, streamlined arcs of three bottle-nosed dolphins dived, one after the other, back into the shimmering waves.

For several delighted moments she watched them surfacing and submerging, envying their agility and power.

Freedom beckoned as she tripped down the steps to the swim platform and stood there beside the life raft.

One step, she thought, dry-mouthed, gathering up the courage to take it. One step and she'd be as free as they were...

Kane had slept too heavily. Normally he was awake before the radio alarm disturbed him, but the World Service was broadcasting the usual troubles on distant shores, floods in Asia, melting tarmac from the heatwave at home.

Pulling on dark bathing trunks and throwing a casual short-sleeved shirt loosely over the top, he raked his fingers through his hair, thrust his feet into open mules and, feeling he could kill for a cup of coffee, made his way up to the galley.

Revived by the first few sips of caffeine, he poured a cup for Shannon and took it down to her cabin, opening the door when she failed to respond to his increasingly loud knocks.

'Shannon?' The deserted, unmade bed brought his attention to the transparent sliding door of the equally deserted shower. 'Shannon?'

How could she be up? he wondered, frowning. He would have seen her. Unless, of course, she had already gone up on deck.

Abandoning the cup and saucer on a vanity unit and checking the smaller cabins each side of the gangway, something moved him quickly up the stairs and back through the vessel, brought him leaping up the steps to the upper deck.

She wasn't on the integral sun bed forward of the helm and a glance over the windshield to the sun pad down on the bow showed him that she wasn't there either.

'Shannon?' An anxious survey took in a panorama of sea and sky, of rocky scrub above an inaccessible beach. Well, almost inaccessible...

Going hot and cold, he could just make out the treacherous path above the shingle. Good grief! She *wouldn't*! 'Shannon!' Panic was a stranger to him but he felt it now, and wanted to kick himself again for the things he had said last night. 'Shannon!'

A movement in the water caught his attention. Dolphins, he realised, counting two—no, three of them, barely breaking the surface, some way out off the stern of the boat.

Suddenly, further in, close to the yacht, he glimpsed the pale dipping head and the smooth limbs cutting through the water.

The damn-fool girl had been swimming with the dolphins! he realised, his shoulders sagging, racing down to the lower deck just as she was pulling herself back up onto the boat.

Relief that had seemed almost to weaken him on seeing her up there on the flybridge was dissolving beneath the twin emotions of shock and something raw and more fundamental that shook him to the core.

She emerged onto the swim platform naked, as lithe as any mermaid, and as alluring. The water as she stood up ran in rivulets down her body, while her blonde hair, plastered to her skull, hung over her shoulders in matted strands.

Then she looked up, saw him standing there on the steps above her, and he could tell from those widening eyes, the open circle of her mouth, that she uttered a small, inaudible gasp.

For eternal seconds, it seemed, they stared at each other. She appeared, he thought, utterly transfixed by his presence. But the beauty of the whole woman seemed to tip him off his axis, making his head swim, rocking his senses as his eyes touched, savoured, devoured her; the pale flesh of her shoulders, the small but perfect breasts with their tight pink peaks, the gentle curvature of her waist and hips, and at the juncture of her thighs that wet triangle of darkened hair…

He felt his body harden, throb with excruciating tension. What the hell was she trying to do to him?

Angrily he stooped to scoop up the bath towel he had only just noticed lying on the deck. Didn't she realise he was only flesh and blood?

'Here.' The towel left him with more force than he realised so that she almost reeled backwards in catching it. 'For goodness' sake! Put something on.'

Stung by his anger, clutching the towel to her, it was as much as Shannon could do to meet that hard, intrepid gaze, prevent her voice from faltering as she said, coming up the steps, 'Why so shocked?' She was surprised at how blasé she managed to sound, how well she was able to mask how shaken she was, seeing him there behind a mocking little smile. 'That daunting immunity in danger of crumbling, Kane?'

As she made to sweep past with her head high, all the power on earth couldn't have prevented him from reaching out to stop her, and she gave a small cry as he roughly caught her arm, swung her angrily to face him.

'What the devil did you think you were doing?' He could feel a pulse beating at his temples, feel his fury threatening to undermine his control. 'Do you know what I thought when I couldn't find you? When I first saw you out there in the water?' The careless attitude, he noticed, had been replaced by something that looked remarkably like…what? Embarrassment? Alarm? He wondered, surprised. So parading herself naked in front of him wasn't something she was as comfortable with as she would have him believe. 'Why the hell didn't you tell me before you took off?'

'Let me go!'

'No.' His fingers bit into her arm as she tried to squirm out of his grasp. 'Answer me first!'

'What would you have done?' she tossed back, wincing, so that he relaxed the pressure slightly. 'Stopped me?'

'Probably. Or at least insisted that you didn't go off swimming unaccompanied.'

'Why? So I didn't come to any harm?' It was a derisive little taunt born out of wondering if he cared when he clearly didn't, and from being so affected by his earth-shaking virility. He looked wild, she thought; unshaven, with his hair all tousled and that linen shirt he had thrown on over his bathers unbuttoned so that she could see his powerful chest and the crisp dark hair that ran in a line right down over his sinewy waist and stomach. 'Or was it just in case it was in my plans to try and get away?'

'You'd have to be stupid to have attempted that,' he commented, more controlled now, 'and both you and I know you aren't that, don't we, Shannon?'

'Do we?' With a little extra force she managed to shrug off his restraining hand. 'I thought sense was the last thing you thought I had!'

His expression was pained with an intensity of emotion she couldn't fathom as his eyes raked over her face, following the path of the rivulets down over her shoulder so that her spine stiffened and her breathing quickened as she felt their tangible heat sweep over the pale, tantalising curve of her hip, the smooth outline of one creamy buttock.

'They're wild creatures,' he stressed, ignoring her pointed comment, his voice hoarse from the ache in his belly of wanting to run his hands over that satin-soft flesh so that he had a job keeping his mind on what he was saying. He prayed she didn't notice how aroused he was. 'You could have sustained bruising at the very least.'

'But still far less painful than with any civilised creature! At least with animals it's only physical—and you know exactly where you are!'

She had been hurt and deeply, he realised, trying to force

his thoughts back onto a more advisable track. Even now she was hurting inside. Nevertheless, he couldn't help his interrogative tone, guessing it sprang purely from sexual frustration, as he demanded, 'Do you always do exactly what you want? Regardless?'

Is that what he thought?

Above them a gull wheeled, and the timbers of the boat clicked and creaked, expanding in the morning heat.

'Why not?' She shrugged. 'I'm the last of the big spenders. A pleasure-seeker! Wasn't that what you called me once, Kane? Pleasure for pleasure's sake? You should try it some time. It might loosen you up a bit!'

'You think I need loosening up?'

Common sense warned her not to keep provoking him like this, but his opinion of her and her hurt pride wouldn't let her give it up.

'I don't have to think—I know! You condemn me for what you think I am, but you're the same as every other man I've ever met. Only you're such a hypocrite because you pretend you aren't! You're dying to make a pass but you don't dare because it would be such an affront to your oh, so valuable pride! Apart from which, you're my father's employee—or should I say his lackey?' She wanted to belittle him, lash out at him as he—as the world—had lashed out and belittled her. 'You wouldn't want to do anything to jeopardise your position with him, would you? Not after walking out on him and then crawling back again. Don't you think your credibility's just a little bit dented? I'm surprised you even think you've got any left!'

Under the canopy of the deck now, she would have swept around the table, but Kane was too quick for her, and she gave a startled cry when the daunting obstacle of his body blocked her way.

'So I'm a hypocrite, am I? A sycophant. Your father's lap-dog.' He spoke with a silky-voiced menace, his hand coming up to catch her chin none-too-gently between his thumb and forefinger. 'And you think my so-called pandering to Ranulph would really stop me from having what I wanted if I were interested enough to want to try?'

She had asked for this, she realised, berating herself, wishing now that she had kept her mouth shut, holding her breath as that broad masculine thumb ran over the soft swell of her lower lip, the action sensual, arousing her, even as it humiliated. Involuntarily, her pale lashes came down to block out the hard derision in his face.

'You think you hold the keys to seduction, Shannon? Do you always call the shots? Think that playing around with men's egos is some sort of game?'

No, she didn't. Of course she didn't! her brain screamed hectically, a rising excitement overriding fear as she became vibrantly aware of the heated musk of his body, of those dark dilated pupils and the cogent force of his dominant sexuality.

This male-female connection was a lethal cocktail of the senses, stronger than any she had experienced before. It was dark and drugging and powerful, as elemental as those dolphins that had rocked her with their power and speed and litheness, as fundamental as the universe and the pull of the sea.

An unconscious glance downwards showed her how aroused he was, although she needn't have lowered her eyes to know that. That flush across his cheekbones and the heavy rising of his chest were evidence enough.

Oh, cool, clever Kane! Not so invincible after all! her brain clamoured, though she could find no words with which to taunt him, feeling the cool peaks of her breasts suddenly tightening unbearably, the tension in the pit of her stomach billowing into an acute ache.

'Congratulations. So I'm human after all,' he breathed, dangerously softly. 'Now, go and put on some clothes before I forget how civilised I'm supposed to be and show you what fooling around with a wild animal is really like!'

Hurting, grossly humiliated, she fled.

CHAPTER FIVE

IT HAD been a gloriously sunny morning with a clear, corn-flower-blue sky. Now fluffy white clouds had begun to drift in off the horizon, accumulating over the forested mountains above the coast.

Lounging, eyes closed, facing the sun, on one of the long upholstered benches on the upper deck, Shannon was conscious of Kane vacating the helm, aware, above the burr of the engine he had left coasting, of his swift, easy movements as he did something at the fridge and barbecue unit behind his seat.

All morning, since that humiliating interlude, she had made it more than obvious that she didn't want to communicate with him any more than she had to and, surprisingly, he had respected her wishes, giving his concentration solely to handling the boat.

At intervals, however, for the forty minutes or so that she had been lying there, she had been unable to stop herself stealing covert glances at him, at his uncompromising profile, at those broad shoulders, rippling with strength beneath that soft white T-shirt he wore.

She had found herself wondering again about the woman who had accompanied him on his outward journey and why he had left her in Barcelona; wondered, with a small kick of resentment, how serious their relationship was. Although it didn't necessarily have to be that serious, did it? Not when there were probably scores of woman who would be only too pleased to take a business-pleasure cruise with him—with the emphasis on pleasure, she decided, her imagination running riot. They were probably queuing up to share a bed with him down there in the master suite!

'Here; I thought you could use something cool.'

Carried away by her thoughts, she gave a small gasp on opening her eyes to see him standing there above her, holding two tumblers of something red and decidedly thirst-quenching.

'Thanks,' she murmured appreciatively, sitting up and taking one from him. 'What is it?'

He sat down on the other end of the bench on which she was lounging, his arm casually outstretched across the back of it. 'Fruit juice, bitters and a dash of grenadine.' He smiled. 'Not at all potent.'

Unlike you, she responded silently, because against the blue of the sea and sky he looked like the god of virility with his strong and striking bone structure, his powerful torso and, exposed by the T-shirt and dark fitted shorts he was wearing, his sinewy, hair-darkened limbs.

She wondered what it would be like to feel the crispness of his body hair against *her* body, and quickly she dropped her gaze, grateful that her own hair falling forward partially hid her face as she sipped the delicious punch through the cubes of ice that chinked pleasantly against her glass.

'How do you feel?' He was studying her so intently that she felt herself grow uncomfortably hot beneath the white beach cover-up she wore over her panties, which she had laundered with her bra the previous night in the vessel's washer-dryer.

It was a wide-necked garment with a beaded fringe around the hem and *Ocho Rios* printed across it, and rather more than she would have chosen to wear when sunbathing. The wardrobe, though, hadn't offered up anything else. Not that she would have worn anything belonging to one of his girlfriends as personal as a bikini if it had! she thought fiercely. And she certainly wasn't going to sit there in her bra and panties!

Those eyes, however, were disconcerting, regardless of how genuinely concerned they seemed, and she caught his drawled remark as she glanced away. 'I must say you look better. You've more colour in your cheeks today.'

'What do you expect?' she returned, looking coastward to the whitewashed houses of a hillside village nestling beneath the pine-clad mountains. 'Being press-ganged into helping you crew?' But she had done nothing so far in the way of assisting him; nor had he asked her to. Perhaps, she thought, he'd decided she wasn't up to it after all!

'Don't pretend you aren't enjoying yourself just a little,' he argued, looking faintly amused. 'That rather adventurous swim this morning really captured the spirit of someone here against her will.'

Dammit! Why had she been so tempted into doing it? she wondered, having already guessed that he would use those moments of weakness against her at some stage.

'Only because, as you said, I'd have been stupid to try and get away. And if there's something I know how to do, Kane,' she uttered, still trying to save face, 'it's enjoy myself under any circumstances.' Well, wasn't that the kind of answer he would have expected from her?

Silently, though, she had to admit that she did feel better this morning—better than she had felt in weeks—and decided that it had more to do with the sea air and sunshine than with any altruistic act on Kane's part.

'Is that what you were doing in Milan?' He took a long draught of his own beverage. 'Enjoying yourself?'

Her glass suspended halfway to her lips, Shannon looked at him dumbounded. 'How did you know I was in Milan?' she asked charily.

He was sitting there, impervious to the impact his glaring manhood was having upon her, enjoying his drink, his fingers long and dark against the cold condensation of the glass.

'I'd been tracking you for months. I traced you there, but

your landlord said you'd already left weeks—months!—before. What were you doing there?' he repeated, with more tenacity infusing the deep voice now.

She shook back her hair, felt his eyes track the alluring little gesture, touch on the fine lines of her profile, the pale, smooth column of her neck.

'I did a bit of modelling,' she told him, trying not to show that she was affected by it. 'When I wasn't doing that...I studied.'

'Studied?' A masculine eyebrow arched at her declaration. Now, that had surprised him! 'Studied what?'

She shrugged, took another draught of the cooling punch and, irked by the scepticism she had detected in his voice, suggested, 'How to rebel against the unrebellable?'

'There's no such word.'

The briefest smile touched her mouth. 'There's no such subject.' In fact it was qualifications in business studies and business management which she had worked so hard to attain, and which she had secured with the highest grades, although she didn't tell Kane any of that. 'You think I'm just a rebel too, don't you?' she challenged dispiritedly instead. 'Like my father. Just like everyone else.'

He seemed to be weighing up her question because he took his time in answering. 'Wasn't it Lincoln who said, "A little rebellion now and then is a good thing"?'

'Jefferson,' she corrected promptly, and saw his head dip in acknowledgement, the hard lines of that fascinating mouth curl in faint amusement as though he had known that, and had been merely testing her. A meeting of intellects, she thought with a sudden, ridiculous and almost painful yearning, and one in which she was relieved not to have been found wanting. 'And I learned to fly.'

'To fly?'

Not so sceptical now, she thought. In fact he looked almost thrown by this piece of information.

'Did you get your licence?'

Under the tunic her shoulder moved in a little throwaway gesture. 'For what it's worth.'

'For what it's...' Something flared in his eyes as he sat forward, incredulity quickly turning to disapproval. 'What was it? Just another flight of fancy—if you'll excuse the darn pun? A way of alleviating boredom? What are you going to do with everything life offers you, Shannon? Just throw it all away?' He was sitting with his forearms resting on his big, bronzed thighs, gripping the glass he held between them with both hands, judging, looking exasperated with her. 'With your obvious talents and intelligence I would have thought by now you would have wanted to channel them into something a little more useful. Do something more practical with your life.'

Something more practical with her life!

She could taste the dust in her mouth, smell the stench of disease in her nostrils and feel the suffocating, almost unbearable heat...

She wanted to toss back at him that she knew more than he ever could about being useful; throw at him just how *practical* her self-imposed exile had been. But silence, she'd learned long ago, ensured privacy, and privacy was what she craved next to real friendship, next to love. People got bored if they couldn't find out anything about you; they left you alone. But disclosing anything about herself to anyone could result in media interest in her flaring up again, and the tabloids would have another field day—and at her emotional expense. At best they might report that she was courting publicity just to salve her own conscience. At worst, they might hound her; hold up to public ridicule all that she was trying to do...

'Alleviating boredom's the privilege of the mega-rich, Kane, but you wouldn't know about that, would you?' she uttered with mock-sweetness instead, getting up and dumping her glass on the cover of the barbecue unit before going over to stand by the rail.

The hillside village was gone, lost behind the bulk of headland around which they had drifted, and now only the mountains rose steeply above the coastline, darkly forested, cloaking secrets.

'I'm not sure I'd want to,' he said.

'Everyone wants to,' she stressed with the breeze teasing her hair, her pale flesh exposed where the tunic had slipped seductively off one shoulder. 'If they don't, they're either abnormal or a liar. But keep playing up to my father.' She couldn't have withheld that if she had wanted to. 'You might get there one day.'

Watching her from behind, Kane felt all his pulses move into overdrive. He'd been with Sophie when she had bought that tunic in Jamaica, but for all her prettiness and femininity, she had never filled it in the way Shannon did. There was something about this girl, the way she looked, the way she spoke, the way she moved, that filled him with a potent elixir of conflicting feelings that went beyond the physical, which continually threatened to undermine the self-possession he prided himself on, and he didn't like it.

'You're a real cynic. Do you know that?' he breathed.

The jangling beads of the tunic parted over her silken thighs as she turned around, resting her elbows on the rail, and tension gripped his insides, his mouth going dry as the action brought his attention to the gentle movement of her breasts beneath the soft cotton, and to the fact that she wasn't wearing a bra.

She looked tense—keyed up—all of a sudden, he thought, as though she had only just become conscious of her provocative pose and what it might be doing to him, he considered, before she slipped her arms down off the rail, murmuring, 'It's been mentioned once or twice.'

Dark lashes lifted as he dragged his gaze from that allur-

ingly bare shoulder. 'What happened to the boyfriend?' It was
something he had wanted to find out since he had first spoken
to her in Las Ramblas.

'Boyfriend?' Her voice was hesitant, guarded.

'The one you moved in with?'

'Moved…' She broke off, frowning, and just for a moment
he wanted to grab her fickle little wrist, pull her down over
his knees and treat her to the spanking he'd suggested yesterday. How the hell could she pretend not to know what he
was talking about?

Restraining every instinct that seemed to be driving him
crazy, huskily he rasped, 'Have there been so many you can't
remember?' I'm talking about the one who was important
enough to throw up your lodging for when you were in Italy.'

'Oh, Piers!' She gave a tense little laugh and looked about
to add something more, but their mutual clash of eyes seemed
to sober her mood, holding her there with her bright, luscious
lips slightly parted as though she were caught by the same
devastating sexual pull that was straining all his limitations.
'Piers was the one I was in Peru with.'

'Ah!' he breathed, as though that clarified everything.

Only it didn't, Shannon thought, mentally giving herself a
shake out of the mesmerising impact of his masculinity. She
had never lived with Piers. Well, not in the way that Kane
was accusing her of anyway. It was Piers and his wife who
had helped her when she had fled England and the Press,
helped her to recover her self-esteem, guided her towards doing something she really wanted to do, something worthwhile…

'And where is dear Piers now?'

His derogatory tone put her on the defensive, making her
more determined than ever not to give him the satisfaction of
knowing the truth. She gave another little shrug and, moving
away from the rail, said nonchalantly, 'We went our separate
ways.'

'Naturally.' Finishing his drink, he reached across and put his glass down on the smooth white surface of the unit beside hers. 'Poor Piers,' he remarked, and stood up. 'I feel almost sorry for him. Especially since he can be so easily forgotten. Do you remember any of them, Shannon? Or are they just a long, blurred line trailing in your wake?'

A gust of wind swept over the deck, rustling the pages of the magazine she'd left lying on the bench, making her shiver, although that had more to do with Kane's obvious contempt than the cooling breeze.

Softly, without thinking, she murmured, 'I remembered you.'

A cloud had crossed the sun, dragging the light from his face as he stared down at her, those steely eyes guarded behind the dark sable of his lashes.

'Am I supposed to be flattered?' he said, his voice husky, surprisingly so, yet derisive too.

Of course. His mind was still closed against her and she had done nothing to try and improve his harsh opinion of her. But why should she have to? she asked herself. Wasn't he shrewd enough to tell what sort of person she was? she reasoned wearily, wondering why, after all these years, it seemed so imperative to her. Would no one give her a chance? Would they—would *he*, especially he, always judge her on what the papers had so wrongly and cruelly printed about her? On what her *naïveté* and her trusting nature had unsuspectingly led her into?

Desperate, however, to know something that had been eating away at her since the previous evening, she heard herself asking, 'What about the girl this little number...' scarlet-tipped fingers tugged at the tunic '...belongs to?'

He was moving back to the helm, but glanced over his shoulder, frowning. 'What about her?'

'Does she mean a lot to you?'

'Yes, she means a lot to me,' he answered, without any

hesitation, causing Shannon's stomach muscles to clench painfully in response.

'Are you going to marry her?' Damn it! Why had she even dreamt of asking that?

'*Marry* her?' Surprisingly then, he laughed, showing teeth that were strong and white against the healthy olive of his skin. 'No,' he murmured with equally surprising conviction, checking something on the instrument panel. 'I'm not going to marry her. Why?' Stooped over the controls, he was looking at her quizzically, she noted, abashed, as though he was aware of the way her whole being had seemed to relax when he answered her, how her breath had seemed to leave her lungs as though on a sigh. 'Are you sizing me up for your next conquest? Because if you are, forget it,' he advised drily. 'I always make a point of steering clear of very lovely but definitely overindulged young women like you.'

'Of course you do,' she smiled, hurting nevertheless, and went below then so that he wouldn't realise how much.

The weather turned squally that afternoon. The winds increased, making the sea unusually choppy and bringing short, sharp showers that soaked the decks and drove them both inside, so that Kane was forced to find a safe anchorage for the night much earlier than anticipated.

'Why don't you relax?' he suggested, coming into the saloon before dinner after mooring that evening, because she had instantly dropped the emery board she'd been using into her make-up bag and jumped up before he could join her on the soft U-shaped leather settee. Deftly he caught her wrist as she tried to flee.

'Let me go!' Panic heightened her voice when she realised she wasn't going anywhere. 'I'm not spending any time with someone who's constantly trying to humiliate me.' She had avoided him as best she could since that little scene on deck that morning, eating alone and staying out of his sphere, ashamed of the way he could still affect her when everything he said seemed to be designed to hurt her.

'Humiliate you?'

Even in those casual clothes—dark chinos and a dark tailored shirt—he oozed pure sophistication. He had obviously showered too because his hair was still damp, she noticed, and he smelled tantalisingly fresh.

'By dragging me onto this thing! Taking your frustrations out on me whenever you get the chance! Hasn't it dawned on you that you might possibly be breaking the law? That I might press charges for kidnap?'

Her eyes were glittering like gemstones and there was an angry flush tingeing her flawless complexion, he noted, his mouth moving wryly as he contemplated her question. 'Yes...and no.' And when he saw the query darken those lovely eyes, 'Yes, I probably am breaking the law,' he elucidated, 'but I don't think you'll press charges because I don't think you were very happy where you were.'

Angry defiance animated her perfect features as she wrenched free from his restraining hold. 'You're very sure of yourself!'

He watched her massaging her wrist where his fingers had pressed, saw the white marks start to fade as the blood returned.

'Did I hurt you?' He hadn't intended to. 'I'm sorry. But as I said, I didn't think you looked particularly happy—and most definitely not as strong as you should be. One bend and you looked as if you'd break.'

'Well, I wouldn't have,' she assured him, unable to cope with continually being lured into wondering if he cared—even just a little bit, adding confidently, 'I'm pretty resilient, Kane.' She had had to be, she thought, to survive the scandal and the finger-pointing she had had to face for making the mistake of caring for someone, trusting too deeply; for rebelling in the first place against the parental tyranny she was unable to endure.

'Maybe, but you're not entirely invincible, Shannon,' he stated as she started to move away. 'And I'm not forcing you to go home. That's a decision you'll have to make for yourself eventually. But your father isn't well—'

'Not well?' She had reached the galley steps, but turned round now, looking strikingly lovely, he thought, even in her red 'bull' top and the white cropped leggings she had obviously found in her cabin. Her eyes were large and anxious, though, and there was a crease between her fair, perfectly arched brows. 'I asked you how he was. You didn't say—'

'Oh, it's nothing life-threatening,' he cut in, wondering if it was relief that made those slender shoulders sag as she came back to flop down a safe distance from him on the opposite settee. 'But it could be if he carries on the way he's going. Worrying about what's happened to you—on top of everything else.'

'What do you mean?' she queried, through her aching hope that perhaps Ranulph Bouvier might possibly have some feeling for her after all. 'What do you mean—everything else?'

'I mean the massive loss of revenue the company's sustained during the last few years. Ranulph was in danger of having to pull out. Didn't you know?' he enquired, frowning.

'No...' Before she left, she had been aware that profits were down, but it was nothing, she had suspected, that couldn't be stemmed without a pulling-in of belts, and a new strategy to support future projects that she knew Ranulph was putting in place, though he had never actually discussed company matters with her.

'For goodness' sake, Shannon! I know it means very little to you beyond financing your extravagant lifestyle, but I would have thought even you would sooner or later show some inclination to care.'

Shannon flinched as though from a whiplash, because, of

course, she thought bitterly, she cared very much. It was true that it was the company that had provided her with the privileged existence Kane had so scathingly referred to, but it was also what had financed her education, given her opportunities—reluctant though she had been to acknowledge them at the time—that other people of her age could only dream about. It was also what her mother during her short life and in her own way—as well as her father—had contributed to, worked for. For those reasons alone, its success or failure meant a great deal to Shannon.

Ignoring Kane's remark about not caring, determinedly she pressed, 'What else should I know?'

From the set of that rugged jaw he obviously thought that she shouldn't even have needed to ask.

'He was heading for big trouble,' he stated grimly. 'One hell of a fall. His new strategy didn't work. I knew it wouldn't. I saw it coming—years ago. He wouldn't listen to me—or to reason. That's why I left.'

'That's why…' Was he really that clever? That far-sighted? A little shiver ran through Shannon as she guessed that he probably was. 'So what happened?' she prompted, and then a little more acidly, 'Did he welcome you back on to the board with open arms for another prediction on the future?'

He acknowledged that little sneer with only the barest movement of an eyebrow.

'Your father contacted *me*—and because he was desperate,' he told her roughly.

'He must have been,' Shannon returned, regretting her tasteless attempt at sarcasm even as it slipped out because his revelation had left her metaphorically winded. So he hadn't come crawling back to Bouvier's. Ranulph had approached *him*. Not just an ex-menial, but also one who had dared to walk out on him. It was unheard of!

'He wanted my advice because he knew I knew his business inside out—hoped I could help him pull it together.'

I should have been there, she thought, and knew she would have been if her father had once told her he'd needed her instead of refusing to acknowledge her capabilities, instead of continually belittling and criticising everything she did.

'And have you? Helped him pull it back together?' Although she still couldn't keep the resentment out of her voice, there was genuine concern behind her question.

'Perhaps if you hadn't been so conveniently absent while all this was going on—taken some interest in what was happening—'

'I did. Or I tried to,' she informed him heatedly, 'but perhaps you might not have noticed, my father's never forgiven me for being a girl! He wanted a boy to succeed him—to carry on the business, the Bouvier name. All he's ever wanted for me is to marry me off to somebody *suitable*! He isn't—and never was—interested in my ideas or my opinions!'

Some curious emotion flitted across that strong masculine face, something that made a muscle tug in his jaw and brought his thick black brows together.

Quietly then, he said, 'Tell me.'

For a long moment those blue eyes held his as though he had just asked for a conducted tour of Mercury, and the only sound was of the distant wheeling of a gull somewhere above deck.

'You?' she uttered with a little laugh. 'You'd never get any suggestions of mine past him. He'd find out where they came from, and even if he didn't, if your ideas didn't tally with his, he'd have his way and you'd just wind up walking out again.'

'No.' He sounded so certain, she thought. So unmistakably sure.

'Why?' she queried, and then, rather acidly, 'Is the salary high enough to make you bite your tongue this time?'

It was like continually brushing against nettles with no way of avoiding them, Kane thought, his skin prickling from her constant stinging remarks. He hadn't realised just how bitter she was—how raw—and Bouvier, he was sure, had contributed immeasurably to her attitude. Without displaying any emotion, however, prosaically he said, 'Your father will listen to me.'

He seemed confident, so self-assured, she thought, but he seemed to be waiting, the strength of that meaningful silence, like those keen eyes, inviting her to tell him. And so she did, expressing how she believed they could make their projects more attractive to the buyer, suggesting new and alternative marketing tactics that Ranulph had never believed in trying. 'We've been so sure of our name, we've become complacent and there isn't a company anywhere that can afford to do that.' She went on, outlining other aspects she believed could be given a boost, while Kane listened silently and attentively, not interrupting her as her father would have done before she had even half-aired her views, but giving time and space to her comments—as though they were important to him, as though they mattered.

Which was crazy, Shannon thought, because when all was said and done he was still, at the very most, only one of her father's salaried directors. Ranulph Bouvier would have the last word, no matter what Kane Falconer thought. So what did he care about her opinions counting for anything, just so long as he received his handsome pay-cheque at the end of each month?

Even so, no one had ever really made her feel as though she was worth listening to before, not genuinely, she thought—remembering Jason—and she liked the feeling, especially when, on finishing her little spiel, she could see that Kane was impressed.

'You're full of surprises, aren't you?' he remarked, sitting there surveying her, totally relaxed, with one long leg resting casually across his other knee.

'Am I?' she whispered, the warmth she could feel stealing through her from his smouldering concentration seeming to creep right down to the tips of her painted toes. 'What did you imagine,' she challenged quietly, 'that I wouldn't be capable of organising anything more taxing than next week's manicure?' And when his only answer was a twitching of that firm mouth, rather tremulously she added, 'Well, there's more where that came from, Kane Falconer.'

'What?' Suddenly he was getting to his feet. 'Intelligent observation?' Broodingly, from beneath her lashes, she watched him move over to the entertainment system and stoop to take a CD out of its case. 'I'm sure there is.' The gull's plaintive cries—farther away now—intermingled with the click of a switch, the whirr of the CD player closing as Kane stood up again. 'Or were you talking surprises?'

'Both.' So he wasn't taking her seriously after all, she thought hopelessly, when he turned round and she saw the amusement curling his lips. 'I haven't exactly let the grass grow under my feet since I left home.'

'I can well imagine,' he murmured, mouth turning ironic just as the strains of Debussy's 'Petit Suite' started to fill the saloon.

No, you can't, Shannon responded silently, wondering why she was hurting so much inside. He had never been anything more to her than her father's business colleague, and yet what he thought about her mattered so much it was almost terrifying. 'You wouldn't say that,' she murmured aloud, 'if you really knew me.'

'Wouldn't I?' That wistful yet seductive note in her voice had Kane catching his breath. He wanted to get to know her—and in ways that would bring that smug little smile to her mouth, if only she knew.

For one long moment he fought against the desire to cross the short distance between them, pull her up off that settee, take her in his arms and embark on the hottest and most inadvisable seduction of his life. He felt the hands at his sides clench and unclench as he struggled to steady his breathing, wishing he hadn't put on that damn music as a diversion. It was far too soft and sensuous for him to imagine he could listen to it and stay in the same room with her.

He swore then, quite viciously under his breath, before striding away and down the stairs to his own cabin, leaving Shannon with the cutting realisation that even the possibility of his getting to know her was objectionable to him.

CHAPTER SIX

THE terracotta roofs of the shops and terraced cafés along the waterfront marked a vivid contrast to the brilliant blue of the sky.

Standing on deck, wearing one of Kane's shirts over borrowed leggings, Shannon was shouting directions to guide him in as he reversed the yacht carefully between the other vessels moored, stern-to, against the quay.

Quickly, doing as he instructed, she tossed the mooring line over the side to the man waiting on the wharf.

'How on earth did you manage to get a mooring in St Tropez?' she had asked Kane earlier, guessing that a berth on its fashionable waterfront wasn't something one could come by easily.

'Connections,' was all he had said drily, so she had had to be content with that.

Now, as he leaped down the steps from the bridge and off the back of the boat to help secure the lines, Shannon's gaze feasted on the agile strength of his body. His bare forearms contrasted darkly with a casual white shirt, while pale tailored trousers hugged the taut muscles of his powerful thighs.

Suddenly, though, he glanced up, his expression half-quizzical, half-aware, and quickly she transferred her attention to the tanned and weathered middle-aged man who was helping them with the lines. He gave her a broad, beaming smile, which she returned with as much enthusiasm, because it was a diversion from that lethal magnetism of Kane's and that disturbingly shrewd mind; because it was uncomplicated, easy.

When she glanced at Kane again he looked surprisingly

grim and, still too aware of him, she made a show of looking uninterestedly away.

The Riviera resort held its own delight in any case, with its rows of sleek white yachts, its promenade and, peeping above the roofs of the white and ochre buildings opposite the quay, the distinctive yellow dome of the clock tower. But it was the opalescence of the water that took her breath away, the purity of the sea and sky with the verdant hills of the peninsula that held her in thrall, so that she had recovered a little from the lure of that potent masculinity by the time Kane stepped back on board.

'I can't get over the clarity of the light,' she commented to him, genuinely affected. The sunlight on the buildings was so vivid, the tones of the environment so stark, that the water threw back a canvas like some impressionist painting, shimmering, bleeding colour, rippling with life.

'Which is why Gauguin, Van Gogh and others like them came, and have been coming here for generations to paint, because they were just as captivated as you are.' And they were still coming, Shannon thought, judging by the easels that were set up by several industrious artists along the quay. 'Do you look at every man as though you want him to undress you?'

His question, totally out of context, jolted her head round, her hair moving like liquid sunlight across her shoulder. 'What?'

'Do you treat every man to the same generous promise you treated poor Stephan to?'

Shannon frowned. Surely he wasn't referring to the simple smile she had exchanged with the man!

Rather offhandedly she said, 'I don't know what you mean.'

'No,' he agreed, his countenance still set in uncompromising lines. 'I don't believe you do. Are you ready?'

It was good to be ashore, to feel concrete beneath her feet

and to wander along the narrow, medieval back streets with their secluded cafés and exclusive boutiques, and she suddenly felt such a lightness of heart that she found herself happily agreeing to Kane's suggestion of coffee.

His choice, as it turned out, was a rustic little delicatessen café adorned with wrought iron and wicker, where a window of continental pastries lured them inside with the tantalising aroma of freshly ground coffee.

'*Deux pains au raisin, s'il vous plaît,*' Shannon heard Kane ordering at the counter as she found a seat in the window, listening as he continued to converse with the waiters. His deep, sexy voice suited the accent perfectly, she decided, while his mastery of the language put hers to shame, and she was the one with the French ancestry!

The two young waiters were laughing congenially at something he was saying, and from their easy manner and the way they kept sending overtly admiring glances in her direction, it was clear that they were talking about her.

'I admire your taste,' she managed to interpret one of them commenting to Kane, while the other tagged on, 'And he doesn't just mean with the coffee!'

Although she didn't catch Kane's reply, warmth suffused her blood, nevertheless, to hear other men expressing their appreciation of her in front of him.

'Do you come here often?' she quizzed when he returned to their table to sit opposite her. It was apparent this wasn't his first visit to the café.

'As often as I can get to St Tropez,' he drawled, with no mention of what had just been said over the counter.

'Aren't you worried that someone might recognise me and your reputation will be shot to pieces?'

'Why should it? We're hardly lovers, are we?' he reminded her.

'Fortunately, no,' she breathed, grateful that one of the waiters had come over with their coffees and a basket containing the raisin-filled pastries Kane had ordered, so distracting his attention away from her and the sudden ridiculous misery she felt inside. Not that he would worry if people did gossip about his being with her—or say anything else about him, Shannon decided. It would leave him unscathed, like the breeze brushing over the leaves of a great sturdy tree. He wouldn't be wounded and scarred by it, as she had been.

'They offered me four of these...' A strong brown hand was reaching for one of the pastries. 'It seems you managed to work some magic with those poor boys behind the counter. However, I've got a goodwill call to make while I'm here and it includes lunch. They're expecting us at midday.'

'Us?' Shannon uttered, flabbergasted, managing to conceal her surprise behind the unthinking smile she flashed the waiter as he finished placing the serviette-wrapped cutlery on the table.

'Yes, *us*,' Kane asserted, a little more irritably. He cast a half-disparaging glance towards the retreating Frenchman. 'You don't think I'm letting you loose in St Tropez without an escort, do you?'

'Why not?' Her hair rippled like silk as she shook her head and laughed, the bright sound bringing the two interested male heads turning in her direction. 'You think I might try to seduce every man I see?'

'I thought you might like the break. Someone else's company other than mine,' he expressed, ignoring her pointed remark. 'Besides, the Coltranes are old customers of your father's. You've as much right to be there as I.'

His statement surprised her. Ranulph would most probably have insisted she amuse herself shopping until his business was finished. Much as she was aching to go, however—to see, speak, to other people—she wasn't too happy being told that it had all been arranged without her even being consulted. Not when she had been given no choice about coming here in the first place!

'I can't,' she said flatly, surprised to feel more disappointed than pleased in having to remind him. 'I've got nothing to wear, remember? I can hardly turn up for lunch at someone's home wearing your shirt and your girlfriend's cast-offs!'

With a softly mocking glance over the dark blue tailored shirt that was several sizes too large for her, casually he broke off a piece of sticky pastry. She had rolled the sleeves back, over and over, to the elbows, and, much as he liked the thought of his clothes covering her soft, delectable body, he had to admit she looked lost in what had been tailored to his broader, far more muscular torso.

'That's no problem,' he said, popping the confection into his mouth. 'This place is bursting with boutiques. I would have thought a girl like you would have a field-day.'

'A girl like me probably would…only…' She placed the pastry she'd taken from the basket down onto her serviette, not hesitant—as he had been on his first visit to France—over the very un-English way of eating from the table. And he wondered, as she fixed him with those baby-blue eyes, put a red-tipped finger to her lips to lick off the sugar with an incredibly sensual flick of her tongue, if she was doing it deliberately just to inflame him. If so, she was doing a pretty good job! 'I haven't any funds,' she said, in lowered tones.

'Haven't…' Still trying to recover from the effect her actions were having on him, Kane stirred his coffee with a deceptively steady hand. 'You're the heiress to a multimillion-pound concern and you're telling me you have no money?'

'That's right.'

She had to be kidding, he thought and, irritated by frustration—by his own, self-imposed restraint—he couldn't keep the disparagement out of his voice as he lobbed back at her, 'Doesn't Daddy always foot the bill?'

His tone was so censuring that it took every effort on Shannon's part not to leap up and walk out of the café, turn her back on his denigrating criticism as she had done with those who had pointed a finger at her before. But this was different. For the first time in her life she felt the need to defend herself; justify her motives; wanted him, if no one else, to look at her and see someone other than the pleasure-loving debutante which the tabloids had labelled her, which he himself had so unfairly judged her to be.

'I don't get any real money of my own until I'm twenty-five—only an allowance,' she clarified calmly. 'I thought my monthly transfer was going through. It wasn't. My father stopped my allowance and I didn't know. I didn't find out until I got back to Barcelona and then I was too unwell to do much about it. The bank withdrew my credit when the regular cash flow dried up.' Because the project upon which she had embarked had taken a lot of her savings, she thought, although she didn't tell him that. And what was left she had had to use to clear her debts.

'You mean you were jet-setting round the world—' incredulity lit his eyes '—spending money—without even bothering to check that there was any available?'

Put like that it did sound pretty irresponsible. But then it hadn't always been possible...

A shoulder lifted beneath the expansive blue shirt. 'I didn't think I needed to. There always was.'

'And you thought that that was the way it always should be, in spite of running off without letting anyone know where you were? Choosing to desert?'

Oh, what was the point? she thought hopelessly, glancing out at a fashionable young woman who was passing the window—like every other woman, it seemed in St Tropez, with a tiny dog. His mind was so made up about her, he'd turn everything she said into the actions of a spoilt brat, so what did it matter if he never knew?

'I didn't desert! I was driven out!' she emphasised fiercely. 'But of course I'd have gone back if I'd known anything was wrong.' At least Kane had been right in believing that about her. 'But I didn't. And financially, I thought I had everything in place before I left Europe. I never dreamt for one moment that my father would cut me off without a penny!'

Tears burned behind her eyes, not from the monetary loss but from simply realising that her parent could plunge her into such financial difficulties just to try and control her, bring her to heel.

'And how exactly had you proposed to live? How were you planning to survive if I'd left you in Barcelona?'

'My friends let their house to me rent-free on a temporary basis while they're working abroad. The cupboards and freezer were stocked. And there is such a thing as working for a living, Kane. I thought you'd heard of it.'

'Strangely, I had.' He folded his arms, muscles bunching beneath the silky hairs, his eyes questioning the glistening depths of hers—the emotion she was determined not to let him see.

'You just never associated it with me.' When he didn't rise to her taunt, she said, 'I was going to get a job—any job— as soon as I was fit, for just long enough to earn the money to get me back to Peru.'

'To Piers?'

'No, not Piers,' she said, sounding quietly impatient with him, adding after a moment, 'Piers is married.'

That never stopped you before. He didn't say it, but the way his eyebrow lifted told her that he was certainly thinking it.

Casually, hiding her hurt behind the twist of a smile, she said, 'I'm more particular these days.'

Something flared in his eyes, some dark retaliation he fought to control and conquered.

'And there I was, tempted by your offer of paying me double to take you back to Barcelona,' he commented, amusement suddenly softening the hard line of his mouth so that, against her will, she felt the dangerous snare of his attraction tightening around her.

'Come on,' Kane advised ten minutes later, taking her elbow as they stepped out of the café.

'Where are we going?'

He didn't enlighten her as he guided her through the narrow pedestrian lane that eventually opened up into a tree-lined square.

Restaurants and cafés spilled tables and chairs onto the pavements, and locals and tourists alike browsed around the numerous market stalls that ran through its centre, assessing fruit and vegetables, looking for bargain gifts that certainly couldn't be found in the small, exclusive boutiques that hemmed its perimeter.

Distracted by all the activity, Shannon offered up a silent, startled query when she realised Kane was pushing open the door to one of the designer boutiques.

'Well, we can't have you going around naked,' he informed her, before pressing her forward into the path of a very sophisticated and glamorous-looking assistant.

'Monsieur Falconer.' The woman's face, as elegant as any ballerina's, broke into smiles as soon as she saw Kane.

He was even known *here*?

'Dress her for me, will you?' he was saying audaciously to the woman in his most charming French, but there was a glint of amusement in the steely eyes that ran over the fine feminine silks and chiffons the boutique was displaying. 'Let her have anything she chooses, and charge it to me.'

'I don't want your patronage, Kane Falconer,' Shannon hissed, needled at being discussed as though she weren't there.

'Well, that's too bad, because it looks like you've got it,' he drawled, his smile mocking her, and just as quickly as he'd ushered her inside, he left.

Flabbergasted, Shannon smiled distractedly at the assistant, but inside she was fuming at Kane. Did he bring the woman who 'meant a lot to him' here and treat her with the same patronising attitude? Was that how he managed to have an account in a shop exclusively for women?

Considering storming after him and telling him just what he could do with his generosity, she was turning for the door when the assistant, asking her charmingly in French if she could help, waylaid her.

Well, why not? Shannon thought, a bolt of sudden mischief making up her mind. He deserved some grief after all the inconvenience he had caused her—the indifference with which he constantly treated her. And he *was* giving her a free hand…

'*Oui, madame,*' she murmured, her smile mysterious, her gaze already picking out several garments that were outrageously exclusive, and carried a price tag to match. 'I think I'll try these…'

Eagerly she went over to select them. *OK, Kane Falconer,* she thought wickedly. *It's pay-back time!*

The bell tinkled softly as Kane entered the shop, the blend of the assistant's perfume and a rose pot-pourri enveloping him with rails of silk and lace in a world that was exclusively feminine.

'*Monsieur Fal-con-ere.*' The strongly accented way in which the assistant addressed him only added to the sensuality of his surroundings. '*Elle est prête pour vous!*' A graceful arm indicated the changing room as she spoke, her declaration of Shannon being ready coinciding with the jangle of brass rings.

The curtain was being pulled back, and as Shannon stepped out of the cubicle into the shop Kane felt his eyes bulging, his whole physiology responding to her.

Her long blonde hair was hooked back on one side with a

silver slide that she had obviously just selected for the purpose, but it was that perfect figure that he couldn't tear his eyes from, swathed, as it was, from top to toe in soft white leather.

The short jacket—pulled over a cropped silver camisole that exposed her slim midriff—was decorated with an array of fine silver chains and buckles. The matching hipster trousers, trimmed with similar fine chains, revealed her amazingly flat stomach with that alluring little navel, and when she turned and started moving towards him he noticed the line of latticed strings criss-crossing the curve of her hip and thigh to the tip of each slender ankle, offering him a tantalising glimpse of her soft flesh beneath, gold against the sensuous sheath of white leather.

'*Monsieur?* You are happy?' Swiftly the assistant reverted to speaking in English, having already assessed that Shannon's French wasn't anywhere near as fluent as Kane's. 'She looks…sensational…yes?'

He felt as if he had been robbed of coherent speech. He had never seen anyone—or anything—quite so stunning in his life. He had to moisten his lips before he could speak, and when he did it was as though something had stolen his breath as well.

'Sensational,' he echoed huskily, while his eyes couldn't seem to get enough of her. He wanted to peel that leather off her body, lay her down on the deep pile of the carpet and love her senseless right here in the shop!

A little *frisson* ran through Shannon as she realised the impact she was having upon him, the way those steely blue eyes were still looking at her, setting her blood on fire. She had the sudden mental picture of uncaging a tiger she had temporarily mistaken for tame, but she shook the notion aside as she stooped to gather up her purchases.

'Are you going to carry my bags?' She smiled brightly as she held them up for him to take from her.

It looked, Kane thought, as though she had bought the shop!

'Oh!' Another bag rustled as the assistant rushed round from behind the counter. 'And your bikini, *mademoiselle*!'

'Bikini?' Kane slanted Shannon a glance that was wry and questioning. She handed him that too.

'Now all you have to do is pay.' Her smile was one of sweet artifice.

So will you, my love, his eyes promised as the other woman bent to deal with the invoice, sending a lick of apprehension and excitement through Shannon's veins. Was that flare of anger in his eyes put there by the amount she had spent? she wondered dubiously, because of course she was going to pay back every penny when she got back home. Or was it because of how she was affecting him? Because of his firm disclaimer about being immune to her when he so clearly wasn't?

Oh, to topple that daunting self-possession! Have him crazy for her as so many other men had been—men who didn't matter—and whose advances she had always managed to stave off…resist.

'Congratulations,' he breathed as soon as they were out of the shop, his mouth a tightly drawn line, although that hard glitter in the eyes that tugged over her was of desire rather than disapproval. 'You've got everything but the whip.'

She laughed and, exhilarated—emboldened by the clothes and the power of her own femininity—she slipped her arm under his, and felt a shaft of pleasure in the bunching of warm muscle beneath her fingers.

Her hair moved softly as she tilted her head provocatively towards his. 'Why do I want a whip when I've got my Kane?'

He smiled wryly at the pun. 'Very funny,' he drawled as they began walking, but she saw the tension in his face and felt the rigidity in his body before he glanced carelessly away.

Everyone was looking at her, she despaired as they made their way back across the busy square, still feeling good in spite of the envying glances she seemed doomed to draw from every woman, and the stark, disquieting desire she saw in every man. One or two of the younger males who passed her even whistled softly under their breath.

'What is it you do to these boys, Shannon?'

So he had noticed, she thought, the censure she saw in his eyes making her stop just short of pointing out that it wasn't only the boys, but the more mature members of his sex who felt it their right to ogle her as well!

'I don't *do* anything!' she returned heatedly, just as one elderly man who hadn't been able to take his eyes off her pushed his bicycle straight into the bumper of a car parked by the kerb.

'Not consciously, no,' Kane agreed. 'It's such a part of you, it's as congenital as that sexy angel hair and those smouldering, baby-blue eyes of yours. You *look* like an angel, but you're a witch, Shannon. You cast a spell over every poor, unsuspecting male who just happens to pass you by.'

'But not over you?'

Dear God! If he could open up and admit it! This pretext was driving him crazy! Her nearness was driving him crazy! The battle for restraint, however, which he knew he was coming very close to losing, made him sound cold—heartless even—as he responded tautly, 'No, not over me.'

A car was waiting for them as they came back onto the promenade, a huge white Mercedes, obviously prearranged, and driven by the man called Stephan who had been there on the quayside earlier.

'Stephan's worked for the Coltranes for over twenty years,' Kane explained from the front seat, as the car climbed the green and flowering hills above the town, 'even before they sold up and joined the growing number of British expats seduced here by the climate and the greater feeling of space that France has to offer. Incidentally, they're friends of mine—in fact, the closest thing to family—as well as business associates.'

His voice held a warning, and Shannon wondered why. Didn't he trust her to behave herself? Did he think that because of her past and the awful things the papers had written about her, she might somehow show him up?

Doubts about her self-worth threatened to undermine the hard-won self-esteem she had struggled to regain after her involvement with Jason Markham. In Kane's eyes, she realised—and probably everyone else's—she was still the girl who had nearly wrecked a marriage and been responsible for the tragic near-death of an innocent mother-to-be. Crazily, though, it was only Kane's opinion of her that seemed to matter to her now, no matter what the rest of the world thought; Kane whom she wanted on her side—only he wasn't—and, sitting behind his broad-shouldered frame, with all her purchases on the seat beside her, she wondered unhappily why he had gone to all the trouble of virtually kidnapping her to try and persuade her to return home. Was it simply for financial gain? Or did he see it as a way of ingratiating himself with Ranulph Bouvier? As a way of getting on—getting ahead in life? she thought, wondering how much her father was paying him for her return.

Instinctively, though, she knew that Kane wasn't a man who needed to ingratiate himself with anyone. Therefore, had he meant it when he'd said that he'd been concerned about her? And if so, why couldn't he have just sent for Ranulph? Simply told him where she was? Instead of which he had chosen to bring her with him. He'd said he hadn't, but had he actually wanted her on board?

She was surprised at the intensity with which she wanted that to be the case. Although was it so surprising, she thought hopelessly, when she had always wanted him, even before that unfortunate episode with Jason? Her friendship with the younger man, she knew now, had been a temporary diversion, a grasping at an ideal. She had felt none of the fire and excitement in her blood that Kane ignited in her without his even being aware of it, both then and—heaven help her!—now.

Had he wanted her with him? she wondered achingly again, even though he had said he didn't, because physically he wanted her, no matter how hard he tried to deny it. So what was responsible for his keeping a tight rein on that rigid self-control? Was it her reputation? Or was it the woman he had brought with him to Barcelona? The woman whom, from what he had said, he didn't treat with quite the same indifference and contempt with which he treated her?

Her spirits were considerably lowered by the time they reached their destination, which turned out to be an elegantly sprawling villa with spectacular views of the coast.

Flowers spilled from its balconies and its creeper-clad white walls stood out against the deep blue of a cloudless sky.

'Come on,' Kane invited, opening her door with a courtesy she knew he would extend to any woman, regardless of what he thought about her. 'Leave your bags,' he advised. 'You can retrieve them when Stephan drives us back this afternoon.'

As the Mercedes pulled away, three figures emerged from the villa: a man and a woman with a little white Scots terrier scampering ahead of them, which conjured up a scene of such domestic togetherness that it brought an unexpected lump to her throat. She would do Kane justice, she promised herself, swallowing emotion. She wouldn't let him down.

'Hello, Baxter, you scamp!' Kane had stooped to pet the excited little Scottie. It was clear he liked the dog as much as the dog liked him.

'Oh, you're adorable!' Shannon laughed, bending down and stroking the wagging bundle of white fur as it suddenly transferred its affection to her.

The couple though were calling the dog back, and Shannon

straightened as they approached and greeted Kane warmly, the woman with a light kiss on his tanned cheek, her husband with a firm shake of his hand.

'I'm Esther Coltrane.' A slender, matronly hand was extended in Shannon's direction. 'And you're...?' the woman prompted, before Kane could introduce them.

'Shannon.' She returned the woman's warm smile, liking her directness, the sincerity in her face that was framed by an expert coiffure of ash-blonde hair. 'Shannon Bouvier.'

'Ah...' her hostess acknowledged, almost cagily, Shannon thought, and just for a moment she saw the mask of congeniality slip, something darken the grey eyes that slid almost involuntarily towards Kane. But then the mask was back in place, and, looking relaxed again, the woman said pleasantly, 'Welcome to our home, Shannon.'

On overhearing, her husband—a well-built man in his fifties with shining silver hair—had no reservations about taking both of Shannon's hands and, clasping them together between his own, lowered his voice to say with mock conspiracy, 'I'm Bart—Bartholomew—Coltrane. Whatever the others tell you about me, I'm afraid it's all true. And I'm very happy to make the acquaintance of Ranulph's lovely daughter.' He was flirting with her in his own way, openly and acceptably, Shannon realised, laughing, as everyone else did, before the man released her, his attention caught by the dog that was still leaping up at her, barking to get himself noticed.

'I know, she's beautiful, isn't she?' her host remarked. 'Far too beautiful for the likes of me and you.' This was said with a rather avuncular wink at Shannon.

'I'm sorry,' Esther said, over the rustling of foliage stirred by the warm wind that swept up suddenly from the dark hills of the coast. 'He's not usually like this.'

Your husband, or the dog? Shannon thought, amused.

'He's never like this with strangers,' the woman continued

apologetically, trying to restrain the bouncing Baxter. 'You must have an affinity with animals or something.'

'Or something,' Kane murmured drily at Shannon's shoulder so that only she caught the cryptic remark before Bart suggested they go inside.

'Well, my angel sorceress.' With their host behind them, scooping up the dog, and Esther guiding them towards the airy sitting room, Shannon felt the hairs rise on the back of her neck from Kane's low, softly flaying tones behind her. 'Is no one—nothing—safe from those witch's charms?'

He was holding her responsible for something that wasn't her fault. That she had no control over, she realised, wishing, as she so often did, that her striking looks didn't always produce such dramatic reactions in people, lead her into the sort of dangerous and threatening situations that she had found herself mixed up in before.

Desperately now, she longed for Kane's submission. To drag him off that high-and-mighty pedestal and make him want her as much as she wanted him. To break through the outer layers of that formidable self-possession he thought protected him from his reluctant yet very real desire for her; see him crumble with that desire, and then watch him eat humble pie when he acknowledged that he had been wrong.

Head held proudly, she glanced back over her shoulder and in response to his question, said meaningfully, 'Only you.'

CHAPTER SEVEN

THE Coltranes had lived on the French Riviera for ten years, moving there when they had sold an extensive piece of land to Bouvier's, Shannon learned when they were enjoying an aperitif in the large and comfortable sitting room.

She was sitting beside Esther on one of the low settees, enjoying the aspect of the garden beyond a pair of open French doors. She could see a table set for lunch, its steel and glassware gleaming; the dark red of a specimen tree, and, through a profusion of pink oleander, the cool, still blue of a pool.

'We've known Kane since he was a youngster,' their hostess went on to inform Shannon when somehow the conversation slid to his background, his parents, and how they had been neighbours back in England before the avalanche that had tragically claimed them while on a skiing holiday in Austria.

'I'm sorry.' Shock showed in the eyes Shannon turned in his direction. 'I didn't know...'

'Didn't you?' he said softly from across the room.

Her gaze held his sympathetically for a long moment. So he, too, had known his share of misery—of pain.

She wasn't aware of the enquiring glance exchanged between her host and hostess and it was Bart, sitting in an easy chair near Kane's, who eventually broke the intimate little silence by clearing his throat and asking, 'So how is old Ranulph these days?'

The question was directed at Shannon and, taken unawares, she found herself fumbling for a reply. She couldn't bear to tell this gentle, harmonious couple that she didn't know how her father was; that she hadn't been home in a long time because they didn't really get on.

Ultimately, it was Kane who came to her rescue with swift and apparently seamless ease.

'He was fine before we left him. Working harder than he should, but we're hoping in the future to give him less to worry about. Aren't we, Shannon?'

His smile was urbane, and she returned it with affected politeness. What he was really saying with that pointed remark, she suspected, was, *I'm taking you home—kicking and screaming if I have to.* And I'll come, she thought bitterly. But you'll be the one brought down before you bend me to your will; pick up your hard-earned reward for services rendered.

No more was said on the subject, however, because light, hurrying footsteps in the hall announced the arrival of another member of the household. It was a slim, dark-haired girl of about seventeen, Shannon assessed, whose flushed and excited features were framed by her mid-length, fashionably untidy hair, and who was turning towards the Coltranes' formidably handsome visitor now as though he were the only person in the room.

'Kane!' She had crossed the smooth wooden floor and flung her arms around him before he had scarcely found his feet.

'Emily.' His lips grazing her hairline, he extricated himself from the hug with impeccable grace. The girl's colour had deepened, Shannon noticed, deciding it was for Kane's benefit that she had poured herself into a dress so short that she looked all legs.

'This is Bart's great-niece,' Esther told Shannon, getting up. 'She's staying with us while her parents are in London.'

'*The* Shannon Bouvier?' The girl's brown eyes widened impressionably as Esther made the introductions. 'What have you been doing lately?' she asked with breathless enthusiasm. 'I haven't read about you for *ages*!'

Silence fell over the room, and Shannon could feel the Coltranes' marked discomfort. Indulgently, however, attempting to soothe their unease, she smiled, concealing her pain to murmur, 'Nothing that newsworthy, I'm afraid.'

'Shannon's been spending time in Peru,' Kane supplied, standing there emanating a raw sexuality that none of the women in the room, Shannon thought, could fail to be aware of. Only Bart was still sitting, pinned there by Baxter, who, having been scolded for trying to cosy up to Shannon, had chosen his master's lap as a suitable place to sulk.

'Peru? Really?' Emily gushed, sending a winning smile towards their charismatic visitor and adding rather enthusiastically, 'With Kane?'

His laugh sounded deeply sexy in the bright, luxurious sitting room. 'No,' he responded succinctly. 'Not with me.'

Of course, he wouldn't want anyone to think they were an item, Shannon thought with aching poignancy, yet, contrarily, she knew a strange excitement deep inside from the satisfaction she was going to derive from seeing him crack.

'I wanted to go with him and Sophie on the yacht, but he wouldn't let me,' Emily told her, the pout she directed at Kane somewhere between that of a calendar pin-up and a petulant child.

'You knew he wouldn't be seeing Sophie for some time and needed a few days alone with her,' Esther placated firmly, and not for the first time, Shannon was sure. Apart from which, taking a lovesick teenager along would have cramped his style, she thought grudgingly, feeling the claws of jealousy ripping through her with such unexpected and lacerating cruelty that her breath caught from the strength of the injurious emotion.

Only Kane seemed to notice, his eyes raking questioningly over the features she held in a rigid, smiling mask. She was grateful when a maid came in and announced quietly to Esther that their meal was ready.

Lunch was an outdoor affair of cold meats, seafood and numerous salads served under a vine-covered gazebo that filtered the rays of the Riviera sun.

'Sit by me?' Emily ordered Kane, whose arm she had made a proprietary claim on since coming outside. 'And Shannon. You sit on my other side. I want to be able to talk to you both.'

So she had, positioning herself at the large round table between Emily and her hostess, while the teenager, in spite of what she had said about including them both in her conversation, monopolised Kane's attention in a way that was painful to watch.

Had she been the same at seventeen? Shannon wondered, feeling almost sorry for the teenager. She didn't think so. But it wouldn't have been any wonder that Kane had had little time for her if she had been!

Now, having treated Shannon to an unexpected inquisition on where she bought her clothes, what brand of make-up she used and whether or not she indulged in aromatherapy, suddenly the girl was exclaiming with wistful effusiveness, 'Oh, Shannon! I wish I looked like you! What's it like to have every man eating out of your hand?'

'Emily!' Esther rebuked in a shocked whisper.

Only a bird, twittering among the vines of the pergola, broke the tense little silence that seemed to have settled over the table.

Fighting for equilibrium, breaking into a sweat despite having discarded her jacket, Shannon murmured, 'Totally inconvenient.' She uttered an affected little laugh, wishing she were somewhere else, trying not to sound as though she minded, as though she cared. 'Sometimes I wish they'd use plates.' She had meant it as a joke, but it came out sounding vain and pretentious.

She despaired with herself for letting this teenager undermine her hard-won self-esteem—her earlier resolve not to let

Kane down—as pain warred with the need to hit back at the girl for putting her in this position, to hit back at anyone who was prepared to judge her just on tabloid gossip, so that she went on, digging a bigger hole for herself with each carefully crafted syllable. 'Table manners they might have, but it's surprising how totally uncivilised they become when they're hungry.'

Across the table she caught the briefest flare of a warning in those steel-blue eyes and covered her shame by giving him a rather sultry smile in return.

Well, what did it matter? she thought with hot colour creeping up her throat, her head lifting higher as she realised that she wanted to provoke him—shake him with her outrageousness. Make people think he was her lover because it hurt so much to realise how it appalled him that anyone should think he was. She just wished she hadn't had to do it in front of the Coltranes, that was all.

'Oh, Shannon! You're so witty!' the girl beside her continued to gush with increasing exuberance. 'And having all those things written about you!'

'Things that were hardly commendable. When you get a bit older,' she said quietly, sadly, seeking self-redemption, 'you'll judge it best not to believe all you read.'

'Oh, I want to!' Emily enthused, with Shannon's reprimand totally lost on her. 'I think it's so...*sensational*!' She cast a glance at Kane after making this last dramatic statement. 'I'd like to cause a sensation myself some day.'

You will, Shannon thought, catching the older woman's further whispered rebuke. The girl, however, took no notice, her attention returning avidly to Kane.

'I must apologise for my great-niece,' Esther expressed, with an elegantly ringed hand coming to rest on Shannon's bare arm. 'I'm afraid she's been overindulged by my husband's nephew and his wife, and has a little too much cheek for her own good.'

'It's all right. We've all been seventeen,' Shannon murmured, sensing Esther's impartiality towards her; that quiet support made Shannon warm to her hostess.

There followed a discussion between them about France, and Provence in particular, while occasionally Shannon caught snippets of the political discussion Kane and the other man were engaged in, aware that the teenager was hanging on his every perfectly enunciated word.

'I've always thought France was the closest place to England—scenically, as well as geographically,' Shannon amended, laughing, sitting back in her seat and drinking in the lushness of the coastal hills above the blue waters of the estuary—a landscape that reminded her so much of home.

'Land of your forefathers?' Esther smiled, aware of Shannon's Gallic links.

Shannon's eyes were misty from comparing this gentle country with the home she realised she was missing more and more with every hour that passed.

She smiled back. 'Perhaps that's why I love it so much.' And perhaps Kane had been right when he'd said that he didn't think she was happy in Barcelona, she thought suddenly. Perhaps he was only doing what she had really wanted all along. Had he known something? she wondered. Seen into her soul and realised the homesickness that burdened her even when she hadn't fully realised it herself?

Such awesome perspicacity caused a little shiver to run along her spine.

A burst of adolescent giggles penetrated her uneasy thoughts before Emily jumped up, scraping the paving stones with her chair.

'I really must have a swim. Come on, Shannon. Let's take a dip together.' She was already unzipping her dress. 'You too, Kane.'

'I'm afraid I have some business to discuss with your uncle,' Kane resisted laconically, his glance up at the teenager one of almost weary forbearance.

'And I'm afraid I don't have any swimwear,' Shannon pronounced with some relief. Which was true, she thought. In a way...

'I'm sure we can lend you something.' It was Esther's voice, generous, accommodating.

'No, really...' What could she say? That, much as she would have liked to swim, she didn't particularly want to subject herself to any more unsettling remarks from the gushing and tactless Emily? Apart from which, she had been wearing someone else's clothes virtually ever since she'd left Barcelona and she'd finally given up doing so back in town today.

'You've forgotten, Shannon.' Across the vacated chair between them, Kane's voice was softly mocking. 'You bought a bikini this morning. You brought it with you. In the car.'

Heavens above! Shannon's heart sank. Why did he have to mention that?

'*Really?*' It was Emily this time, her eyes bright with curiosity. 'Can I see it? Go and put it on.' She was pulling off her dress, the almost modest black two-piece beneath it revealing her slight, still developing figure. 'You can change in my room.'

Blast Kane! Shannon uttered an awkward little laugh. 'It's just for the boat. For sunbathing in...'

'No bikini's just for *sunbathing* in!' Emily remonstrated, and then with her young brow furrowing, 'You aren't afraid of the water, are you?' The question was threaded with a disbelieving little giggle.

That was it! Shannon decided thankfully, grasping at the excuse unwittingly being offered. That was better than saying that the bikini was way, way too skimpy to be seen in.

Barely had she opened her mouth, however, when Kane's deep voice was chipping in. 'Anyone who swims in the sea—

at dawn—with a pod of dolphins is hardly aquatically-challenged.' That ironic mouth told her he had sensed her unease and was playing on it for his own amusement. 'Show them, Shannon.' The ominous scraping of his chair on the stones announced his intention even as he said, 'I'll ask Stephan to bring in the bags.'

What could she do? Shannon wondered, mortified, watching him stride purposefully away to find the chauffeur. Claiming a headache would seem ungracious—if it was believed!—and she certainly didn't want to appear rude after the Coltranes' very gracious hospitality.

Already on her feet, she couldn't look directly at Kane as he came back and dropped the ridiculously small bag bearing the name of the exclusive boutique into her hand, knowing she would only see mockery in his eyes.

'Thanks.' She had walked into this through her own stupidity, she realised, sending him a swift, superficial smile, and now there was nothing for it but to brazen it out.

She emerged from the house wearing a tropical-orange bikini top and a matching rectangle of fabric covering her lower body that exposed one long slender leg as she moved.

She didn't look at him, Kane noted from his seat under the pergola, as, barefooted, she crossed the warm tiled patio towards the pool. Her head was held high on that lovely neck, and she had twisted her hair into a golden topknot that accentuated the taut, fine structure of her face.

At the pool's edge she stood, looking towards the water, where Emily was already performing a splashy front crawl, but without, he felt, even noticing the teenager. There was dignity and poise and an almost ethereal demeanour about this lovely girl, he thought, yet there was tension too, he sensed, in the outline of her delicate jaw, underlying the confident assurance of her beauty. Then she unfastened the pareu, letting it slide from her hips, and Kane felt every masculine nerve leap into throbbing life.

Apart from the orange strings at the nape of her neck and across her back, securing the halter-neck bikini top, the lower half comprised of little more than a beaded thong so that she was standing there virtually naked.

Instantaneously, Kane felt himself hardening and shifted his position to alleviate the sudden discomfort of his clothes, his gaze burning across the smoothness of her naked hips to the line of beads which joined the piece of orange string separating her taut, rounded buttocks.

He gave a low, involuntary whistle under his breath.

'Good grief!' Bart whispered, over the gentle splash of Shannon's slender body breaking the surface of the pool. 'She's like something from heaven, Kane. If she were mine,' he chuckled with an absent glance at the dog who was snoozing contently on the chair Shannon had vacated, 'I'd be tempted to lock her up and keep her all to myself.'

'Yes,' Kane breathed heavily through gritted teeth, wishing he had done just that. He couldn't take his eyes off her as she reappeared to turn deftly into a graceful backward crawl, the long line of her throat exposed, her slender limbs moving effortlessly through the blue water.

How could he keep his mind on anything—let alone business—with this glorious creature flaunting herself in front of him as if he had cast-iron defences? What did she think he was? he wondered despairingly. Superhuman?

Guessing though that that little scrap of nonsense she was wearing had been selected solely for his benefit, Kane felt the impulses that fuelled his hard, hot arousal fuelling his anger as well.

Perhaps that was her intention, he thought. To make him eat out of her hand like all these other fools she had talked about so flippantly; have the satisfaction of seeing him grovel like all the rest.

She hadn't intended, however, to bare herself like this in front of the others, of that much he was certain. Her endeavours to avoid doing so and the subsequent tension he had sensed in her before she had dived into the pool assured him of that.

Through the heat of his anger and an almost unbearable sexual frustration, some gallant part of him admired her courage. She was an intelligent young woman—far more intelligent than he had given her credit for—so if her plan was to seduce him, what was her motive? To see him break, simply because he had said he didn't want her? Because—heaven help him—in spite of all his determination, he was already very, very near the brink. Or was the plan to try and seduce him and then laugh in his face?

A cold unease spread through him as he considered that perhaps she really was just the pleasure-seeking little minx that another man's wife had tried to end her life over. That bending men to her will, without thought or conscience, was how this wayward young woman got her kicks. If that was the case, he thought grimly, annoyed to discover how strongly his reasoning tried to reject that idea, then wouldn't the best course of action be to play her at her own game? Make sure he stayed firmly in the driving seat? Took control?

Gliding to the edge of the pool, Shannon surfaced from a graceful breaststroke and gripping the side, shook the water from her face to see Kane watching her from the pergola with a dark absorption.

Esther was coming out of the house with a tray of beverages, having been inside when Shannon had emerged from Emily's room earlier wearing next to nothing, for which Shannon had been immensely relieved. It hadn't been her intention to shock, but she had, she realised uncomfortably, having seen Bart's jaw drop, felt that sensually charged reaction in Kane.

Now, with Bart's attention on the arrival of coffee, and

Emily floating—quiet for once—on her back, at the other end of the pool, Shannon felt her body begin to pulse from the burning sensuality she saw in Kane's eyes.

He was aroused by her, she realised tensely, but he was angry with her too. That much was clear from the cold calculation she could sense going on in that keen mind. She had embarrassed him in front of his friends and colleagues, and an instinct that was bone-deep warned her, with a shivering certainty, that she wasn't going to be let off lightly this time.

Her hair gleamed wetly under the bright sun, tension bringing her chin up against the sick excitement that was coursing through her. She felt trapped by her own weakening responses, but steadily she held his gaze, refusing to be subjugated by his arrogant masculinity, by the uncompromising purpose she met in that strong face. But then Emily called from behind her, propelling herself in a splashy front crawl to join her, and Shannon caught the barest hint of a smile on Kane's lips—like the acknowledgement of a challenge—that sent a little shiver down her spine before she turned away.

'You really must come again,' Esther told her outside the villa an hour or so later, extending what Shannon was sure was a sincere invitation.

They were standing by the open car, waiting for Bart and Kane to join them. The men were still talking under the sweeping archway of the villa. Emily had chosen to remain there too, instead of accompanying her great-aunt to the Mercedes, and Shannon didn't need to hazard too many guesses as to why.

'I'm sorry about Emily,' Esther reiterated as though picking up on Shannon's thoughts. 'But she does have this frightfully embarrassing crush on Kane. I hope you didn't mind too much?'

'No,' Shannon responded amiably enough, shaking her head, but unhappily she thought, Why should I? I'm not the woman in his life. It was evident, though, that Esther thought she was.

'Bart and I worry about him. He's such a workaholic, though he does seem to thrive on it, and I must admit he certainly looks good for all that drive and ambition.'

They both turned to look at the tall, dark man who was listening patiently to something his voluble host was telling him, while Emily stood gazing up at him like a hungry fawn.

'That's some hunk of manhood,' Esther breathed confidentially, smiling at Shannon. 'Cool as a cucumber on the surface, but a dynamo of complexity underneath. A bit of a volcano, too, if he loses his temper, though I'm pleased to say he doesn't do it very often, and he always makes time for the people he cares about—especially Sophie.'

'Sophie?' A nerve-grazing tension put a crease between Shannon's brows, caused a sudden dull ache to start just above her temple. Did Esther condone multi-relationships between couples? She must do, Shannon thought in amazement, if she thought that *she* was romantically involved with Kane as well.

'She's a lovely young woman now,' Esther was continuing, seemingly unaware of Shannon's unease, 'but Kane's still very protective of her. I expect he told you, she was a mid-life child—a bit of an afterthought in the marriage—and was only eight years old when their parents died.'

'Their parents?' Shannon whispered incredulously.

'A dreadful business,' Esther expressed, clearly referring to the avalanche, but Shannon was hardly listening. So Sophie was...

She gave herself a mental shake, trying to digest the information through the almost irrational pleasure that was coursing through her. His *sister*? And she'd thought...

'Here's Kane now.'

She was battling to pull her features into more composed

lines as he and Bart drew level with them. Emily, she noticed, was clinging possessively to Kane's arm.

'You will come and see us again soon, won't you, Kane?' she implored, only tearing her huge, adoring eyes away from his to utter, rather as an afterthought, 'And you, Shannon. You'll have to get Kane to bring you too.'

Shannon tried to emulate a smile, but it was an effort as she looked into that hard, handsome face and saw the glittering resolve in his eyes. Girlfriend, or no girlfriend, his mind was too set against her for her to kid herself that he would ever bring her here—or anywhere else—voluntarily again.

Sitting beside him this time, in the back of the Mercedes, her various purchases from the boutique stowed away in the boot, Shannon felt the tension stretching like a tight-wire between her and Kane, especially when he said next to nothing to her all the way back to St Tropez, although the few cryptic comments he exchanged with the seasoned Stephan were amiable enough.

'You didn't tell me Sophie was your sister,' she challenged when they were on the quayside, grabbing the last of the bags he hadn't already dragged out of the boot.

'You didn't ask.'

As the car pulled away he turned abruptly, striding past the various yachts along the glistening waterfront with such purpose that she could hardly keep up.

Between the sleek lines of exclusive craft the water was gin-clear, and there was a warm mellowness about the sunlit buildings of the little resort and the peace of the late afternoon that somehow accentuated the conflict between her and Kane.

He was still angry with her, she realised, for the way she had behaved back at the villa, her stomach muscles knotting as he suddenly stopped, extending an arm—courteous in spite of everything—for her to precede him onto the yacht.

She wanted to tell him he could stick his boat—and his precious chivalry! That she was quite capable of getting herself home from there all by herself, thank you very much! Only she wasn't, she thought despondently. Such a luxury as pride wasn't something one could afford when one's credit card had been withdrawn and one's savings eaten up in a bid to help others, so that one couldn't even finance the cost of a flight! And ringing her father and asking him to bail her out was more than her pride was worth. Steeling herself for confrontation, therefore, she stepped reluctantly aboard.

A touch of a button by Kane had the patio doors gliding open and Shannon stepped through them without looking at him, down into the sensuous luxury of the saloon.

The sounds of the day were muted by the doors gliding closed behind them, the deafening silence that surrounded them screaming of an intimacy she didn't want.

Her heart was beating too fast so that she sounded breathless as she said thickly, 'I think I'll take a shower.'

Tripping across the carpet, she had managed the steps into the galley when strong fingers closed around her arm, hindering her progress, making her gasp.

'Not yet you don't!'

'What do you think you're doing?' Fear cracked her voice as she swung angrily to face him, the grimness she met in those dark masculine features tightening the knots in her stomach. 'Let me go!'

'Not until you tell me what you thought that little performance today was all in aid of!'

Shannon swallowed—hard. 'I don't know what you mean!'

'Don't you?' He smiled, the gesture devoid of humour. 'Well, I'll refresh your memory! "It's surprising how uncivilised they become when they're hungry,"' he mimicked, his reminder of the outrageous remark she had made to Emily at lunch bringing shaming colour to her cheeks. 'And then this afternoon—at the pool.'

'The pool?' She was so mortified in remembering it that all she could do to salve her pride was stand there, pretending that she wasn't. 'What's wrong, Kane?' Even before she said it, she knew she was wrong in taunting him in this way, but she couldn't seem to stop herself. 'Surely you weren't shocked?'

Somewhere in the galley a thermostat hummed into life, like an ominous little voice, warning her not to be a fool.

'It's not important how I feel,' he breathed in a seething whisper. 'But Esther and Bart are friends of mine.'

Inwardly, Shannon wanted to curl up and die. Instead, with a toss of her head that brought her golden hair tumbling over the snowy leather of her jacket, she uttered with mock carelessness, 'They didn't seem to mind.'

'Because they're too polite to object when a brazen little hussy decides to flaunt herself in front of them.'

'I wasn't flaunting myself!'

'Really? What would you call it?' His face was blanched with anger, and there was a pulse beating hard at the side of his jaw. 'That little number at the pool was only decent for the beach or the bedroom—and you know it! And after the way you were carrying on today, I'm quite sure there was no doubt left in any one's mind that we were lovers!'

And that was the crux of the matter, Shannon realised. Because it was the last thing he wanted!

'Oh, *dear*!' she spat out with bitter emphasis and, twisting away from him, fled through the galley and down the steps to her cabin, stumbling through the open door before she had realised he had come after her.

'For heaven's sake, Shannon!' His hand reached out for her, yanking her to a halt. 'Can't you see that behaving like this is living up to everything the newspapers ever printed about you?'

'I don't care!' She could feel the sting of tears behind her eyes because the need for his respect—and only his, she realised with excruciating truthfulness—was eating her up inside.

'Well, I do!' he snarled, the hairs she could see curling

above the open V of his shirt rising with each angry breath he drew.

'Why?' she challenged bitterly, realising she had killed what little respect he might already have had for her. 'Because I've tarnished your impeccable reputation?'

'It's yours I'm thinking of, you little fool! When are you going to grow up and start realising that you don't have to be outrageous to get a man's attention?'

'Attention?' Her tongue strayed across her top lip. Was that what he thought she was doing? 'If anyone was after a man's attention it was that pain of a child *I* had to put up with this afternoon! If you hadn't noticed, she was begging you for it!'

'And you haven't been?'

'No!' He had let her go and she backed into the room, the hot denial a strangled little sound in the intimate space of the cabin.

'Isn't that what this…' a jerk of his chin indicated the bags he had brought down for her '…and this…' Another gesture taking in the clinging leather suit '…is all about?'

'No!'

Without looking at them now, he tossed her purchases down onto the bed and moved purposefully around it towards her.

'As you pointed out, we've all been seventeen,' he breathed, reminding her of what she had said about Emily, 'and no mature man's going to fall for the ravings of an infatuated adolescent. But you're old enough to know better, Shannon. You knew very well what you were doing.'

'Did I?' It came out as a squeak as she backed away, only to be brought up short by the hard wood of the vanity unit. She knew what she had been doing all right! Only now she had come face to face with the consequences, she wasn't sure she knew how to handle them. 'I don't know what you mean,' she parried, through suddenly dry lips.

'Don't you?' His mouth curled in a mirthless smile. 'Then I think it's about time I enlightened you.'

CHAPTER EIGHT

A SMALL sound left her and a warning flared in her eyes, but he ignored them both as he dragged her against him, trapping her futile, resisting hands against the warm, solid wall of his chest.

She struggled against his strength, fighting his determined power, twisting her head to avoid his mouth, but his hand had caught in her hair, tugging her head back so that she could do nothing but take the full, punishing onslaught of his kiss.

As his mouth covered hers, she sobbed a stifled protest. Dear heaven! She wanted him! But not like this! Not in anger! she thought hectically, still resisting as he pulled her round, forcing her backwards, down onto the bed.

She might have kept fighting him, fighting the impulses that were screaming through her to give in to her body's weak and reckless desires. But when he came down on top of her, shocking her with the galvanising pressure of his body, she gave a long, shuddering groan, meeting his kiss this time with a sudden ravenous demand of her own.

Oh, heaven! She had longed for this! From the moment she had walked into that office and come face to face with his devastating masculinity she had needed this man to want her...

His hands were inside her jacket, moving over her bare midriff, their pressure and their warmth unbelievably arousing as they made their possessive journey along her ribcage.

Shannon stiffened with tense expectation, her breathing fast and shallow, but when he tugged at the silver camisole and bared her breasts to his febrile gaze, she felt the piercing need in their hardening peaks and jerked towards him with a small cry of wanting.

His mouth was hot and urgent against her flesh, its suckling warmth sending sharp needles of desire down through her loins to the moist heart of her femininity.

She moved restlessly against him, grinding her hips against his, the knowledge of his unmistakable arousal thrilling her, as did the way he groaned when her hands slid under the shirt she had tugged out of his waistband, demanding closer contact with the hard, warm musculature of his body.

She could hear the irregularity of his breathing, feel the raw tension in him that told her just how much he wanted her, while her own senses fed on the scent and feel and taste of him.

He was tugging at the zip of her trousers, his hands warm and firm and possessive, moving now under the pliable fabric, pressing, moulding, arousing her with unbearable sensuality.

'Oh, Kane, please!'

Her impassioned plea dragged him back to sanity. Good grief! What was he doing? He lifted his head to look at her, his hair tousled, his face flushed with the raw need that gripped him.

She looked like a fallen angel, he thought, catching a strand of her disheveled hair and twisting it around his finger. All white and gold and abandoned. Still pure, save for that ravaged mouth that was swollen from his kisses, and those beautiful, slumberous eyes—heavy with desire—which were looking in wanton supplication to him to grant her the passage that would take her to paradise and back again. And heaven knew, he wanted to grant it. But he had brought her here in the first place without her prior consent—no matter how beautiful or provocative she was. Through an agony of frustration, it took every last effort of his will to remind himself of that. And there was no way he was going to give in to this siren's ploy to seduce him just for her own egotistical satisfaction;

to be just another insignificant feather in her cap. Truthfully now, he was forced to acknowledge that he had wanted her too much and for too long for that.

Gently he moved to place a light kiss on her forehead. 'No,' he said firmly, and got to his feet.

Shocked dismay pulled Shannon from her sensual lethargy. 'No?' Her voice trembled as she raised herself up on an elbow, searched his face as he stood there, towering above her. She couldn't believe that he could just stop… 'What do you mean, no?'

She looked so hurt and bewildered that he wanted to drop down beside her and take her in his arms again, drive away the pain that creased her lovely face; carry her with him to the heights of unimaginable pleasure and, in doing so, ease his own raging frustration.

Instead, he forced himself to stay exactly where he was.

'Much as I'm tempted to forget my scruples and the fact that I brought you here, in the first instance, not altogether willingly…' he was surprised at how unmoved he managed to sound; how steady his hands were, calmly tucking in his shirt '…I don't make a point of playing around with the daughters of business colleagues—even such beautiful and willing ones as you, my lovely Shannon. In my experience— as well as being totally unethical—it can sour a good business relationship.'

'You…!' Something sparked in her eyes, making them glitter like dark jewels. He couldn't do this to her. He couldn't! 'Since when did you ever have any ethics?' she choked, tugging down her camisole and sitting up.

'Since five minutes ago,' he told her stoically, noticing how her slender hands were shaking as she yanked her trouser zip back in place.

'You bastard,' she breathed, with angry colour spreading across her cheeks. The fight was back in her, and he preferred her that way. It made him feel far less guilty; much less of a heel.

'I'd have been more of a bastard if I'd gone ahead and taken what you were so generously offering,' he said, 'but I think you have to agree, I've been rather chivalrous in the circumstances.'

Why? Because he didn't feel anything for her? 'Chivalrous!' Shame mingled with frustration, but it was nothing compared to the shaft of pain that that last thought sent lancing through her.

'I think so.' He was standing there like some sort of superhuman, cool and invincible, a mocking smile curving that firm, sensual mouth. 'After all,' he said, with a sweep of dark lashes shading any emotion she might have read in those blue eyes, 'isn't this what you'd planned for me?'

The gaze that shot to his was startled, guarded. Was it? Had she been crazy enough to imagine that she could rock him off his axis and bring him down without bringing herself down with him? Arouse his passion and his masculine animal urges without falling prey to those devastating urges herself?

Involuntarily, her gaze slid down his body, shocking her as it slipped past his tight, lean waist to notice that he was still aroused. He wanted her still, and it didn't matter that she ached for him like crazy! He didn't respect her, or even like her, she suspected miserably. Therefore he would never give in to his desire for her—as he probably believed so many other men had—no matter how badly he wanted to.

'Get out,' she whispered, both humiliated and ashamed.

Cannes was as Shannon remembered it from previous visits: busy, exciting and luxurious. The flower beds were blooming brightly along its palm-studded boulevard, and the opulent buildings sporting their colourful flags testified to a period of grander living that had thrived at the turn of the last century.

She used to think she belonged in this world, she reflected, strolling with Kane along the boulevard, watching the Porsches, Lamborghinis and expensive saloons cruising past the luxury hotels, art galleries and designer shops lining the famous street. Yet she didn't seem to belong. She didn't seem to belong anywhere, or to anyone. A misfit, she thought, turning to gaze, from behind dark glasses, across the rows of pink umbrellas on the crowded beach on their side of the road to the hazy mountains beyond the dazzling sea.

'Why so sad?'

He didn't miss a thing, Shannon reflected despairingly, catching Kane's deep observation at her shoulder.

'You needn't go to all the expense of finding me a hotel,' she parried, evading the question, not caring to divulge her innermost thoughts. 'I may as well stay on the yacht.' He wasn't handing it over until the following morning, which was why he'd suggested putting her in a hotel—suggested that she might be more comfortable. The suspicion that he couldn't wait to get rid of her, however, was causing her almost unbearable misery. 'On the other hand, I could always trade in my watch over there…' She indicated the exclusive jewellery store across the busy road. 'Get myself the price of a flight home.'

'You could,' he agreed. 'But you won't.'

She sent him a questioning look. 'What makes you so sure?'

'Because, for a start, you've already accepted my invitation to this function tonight.'

Only because it was a charity supper that one of Bouvier's old customers was hosting, she thought. Not for any other reason.

'And I've known you long enough to realise you could never resist a good cause. I also know that that watch belonged to your mother before Ranulph gave it to you on your eighteenth birthday. You came into the office that day and showed it to me.'

That's right, she had, she remembered, recalling how she had used it as an excuse to talk to him. She was surprised that he had remembered it, though, reflecting on how afterwards she had felt such a fool in thinking he'd be interested in something so trivial as her birthday.

'Well, then…*you* could always give me the price of a flight home.'

'No,' was all he said, his tone light but firm.

So she was still under his roof—or bimini cover! she thought wryly—and at her own stupid suggestion, the excitement that knowledge gave rise to tempered by the hard realisation that it was because she couldn't bear to leave him.

Dully, she said, 'You're just taking advantage of my situation.'

He uttered a short, sharp laugh. 'That's right, I am.'

'Why?' she enquired pointedly, aware of how the eyes of passers-by were drawn to that aura of power and sexuality exuded by the man beside her; drawn to them both, probably thinking how well they complemented each other. 'To teach me another lesson in humiliation?'

'I wasn't aware that was what I'd been doing.' Through his dark glasses she felt his hard survey of her in the figure-hugging tan waistcoat and flatteringly flared trousers she'd bought in St Tropez and teamed with exquisitely styled, high-heeled tan boots. 'It isn't—and never has been—my intention to humiliate you, Shannon.'

But he had, she thought painfully, thinking of that impassioned scene in her cabin after they had come back from the Coltranes' yesterday, of how her foolishness in hoping to crack that impenetrable shell of his had backfired on her—and in the most shaming way.

She flashed him a bright, but none the less tremulous smile. 'That's nice.' She felt near to tears and had to swallow to force them back, ashamed that he might see them. 'I'd hate to find out what you'd have done if you'd really been trying.'

*   *   *

The function that evening was a glittering affair, held in the ballroom of one of the resort's most exclusive hotels.

'You'll need a dress for tonight,' Kane had said earlier, and it had given her less satisfaction than she had hoped it would, when she'd been picking it out in that little shop in St Tropez yesterday, to tell him that he had already bought her one.

In a soft, diaphanous material, the bodice was white with shoelace straps, cut low over her breasts, the swaying folds of the skirt a blend of white and smoky grey that finished in a tantalisingly serrated hemline. She had swept her hair up into an elegant French pleat, leaving two long gold strands moving softly against her face. At her throat and earlobes she wore fine silver jewellery, which Kane had bought her in town that afternoon, and on her feet she wore the high-heeled silver sandals that she had bought to go with her leather suit.

Now, with the meal over, standing beside Kane with a group of other people, engulfed by chatter and music and light, she recalled how taken aback he had looked when she had come up from her cabin and into the saloon, where he had been waiting for her earlier.

'You look…spectacular,' he had breathed.

Trying to ignore the warm pleasure suffusing her veins, she had murmured in response, 'So do you.'

Discreetly now she stole a glance at that magnificent physique made sleek by the superb cut of a black evening suit, aware that with the added qualities of strong good looks and charisma and a tan that was accentuated by an immaculate white shirt, he had, over the course of the evening, drawn the attention of almost every woman at the dinner.

There had been speeches, presentations and thanks for various monies raised, and now, with nothing left to do but socialise, Shannon turned on hearing her name unexpectedly called.

'Will!'

The tall, mousy-haired man pushing his way through the

milling guests stooped to place a kiss on Shannon's surprised cheek.

'Kane, this is Will Reynolds—a—a friend of mine,' Shannon said hesitantly, before introducing Kane to the other man, and couldn't understand why he was scowling.

Kane nodded in response and felt resentment clamp his jaw. A friend, Shannon had called him. But with no hint of where she had known him from—or why the guy thought he had the right to kiss her, he realised, feeling like demanding some answers before it dawned on him that he had absolutely no right.

'I must say, you look tremendous after the way you were out there,' the man enthused. Kane thought him weathered-looking, even though this Will was probably only his own age, and noticed, as the others they had been talking to started trickling away, the way this newcomer's eyes were feasting on Shannon. 'Piers sends his love, by the way. He's been worried about you. We all have. We've missed you.'

'I've missed you too.' Shannon's smile was wistful and appreciative. 'Tell him I'm all right.'

She sounded appreciative too, he thought, noting how her exquisite features had turned suddenly serious. Was it a serious relationship she'd had with this Piers? he wondered. Even though she had said he was married? Shamefully, he realised he wanted to knock this Will down just for passing on the other man's love.

'How long are you planning on keeping her from us, Kane?' The ingratiating devil was speaking to him now as if he was a long-lost friend! 'Relief-aid pilots this dedicated...' an arm was snaking around her shoulders '...are like gold dust out there in Peru.'

'Relief-aid pilots?'

Shannon swallowed as narrowing blue eyes impaled her with their incredulity.

'And a darn good one,' the other man was carrying on,

oblivious to her discomfort, and to Kane's shocked surprise. 'No mission too dangerous—no job too dirty.'

Against a background of socialising that seemed to blur into a sea of sound Shannon caught Will's words and cringed.

'I'm sure Kane doesn't want to stand here listening to you extolling my virtues, Will!' she chided with a false little laugh, embarrassed by having the work she had trained for— and for which she wanted no praise—being spoken of so laudably in front of him.

'I'm sorry...' The man was looking from one to the other, only then recognising the tension in the air. 'I didn't realise you hadn't....' He directed an apologetic glance at Kane. 'You...knew she flew?'

'Yes,' Kane breathed, and realised that that was probably all he did know about her.

'I'll see you later, then...'

Neither was aware of the man moving discreetly away as two pairs of blue eyes remained locked, one demanding, one in defiance.

'Why didn't you tell me you were doing relief work?' Kane whispered incredulously.

Shannon's fingers tightened around her glass. 'I wasn't looking for your approval.'

'No, but you deliberately wanted me to think the worst about you.'

'No. *You* wanted to believe it,' she reminded him, hurting, gazing sightlessly into a sea of nameless faces. 'I just let you.'

'Like you would have let me make love to you yesterday?'

A pulse started thrumming at the base of her throat. She started to make some unthinking reply, but someone came up to chat to him just as someone else grabbed her attention, drawing her away, so that she didn't get the chance to speak to him alone until much later.

'Come on,' he said eventually, finding and dislodging her from a group of admiring young males from whom she had been wanting to break free. 'I'm sorry if I'm spoiling your fun,' he added somewhat offhandedly to the others, 'but you won't mind if I take the lady home. She's got an early flight in the morning.'

He wasn't asking for their permission. She could tell that from his face as well as his tone and would have said something, except that she was weary of making conversation, and was only too pleased to be leaving.

They were moving through the bar area towards the reception desk when she suddenly heard the voices. A little bit too loud. A little bit the worse for drink.

'...that company's finished anyway. It would have been washed up already if it had been left to the high-and-mighty Ranulph. Putting a third of his workforce out of jobs. Cutting corners to keep his own pocket lined—jeopardising safety, importing materials that weren't up to scratch.'

Shannon was already headed in their direction when she felt Kane's light touch on her wrist. 'Leave it, Shannon.'

She ignored his soft command, her jaw set squarely as she moved over to confront the man who had been speaking, and who was sitting with two other men on the high stools at the bar.

Kane watched her go. She had never looked stronger or more vulnerable, her dignity evident through her fragile loveliness, her complexion flawless, save for that small fading bruise she had suffered at the hands of those demonstrators and which only seemed to draw more attention to her perfect beauty.

'For one thing,' he heard her saying, 'the company in question never has, nor ever will, jeopardise public safety for the sake of financial gain, and accusations to the contrary could well be tantamount to libel. And for another, if some of the workforce asked itself now and again what it could do for the company instead of what the company could do for them, perhaps they would have a little more to applaud and a little less to whinge about.'

For a moment the men were shocked into silence, until the loudest one among them, looking red-faced and aggressive, snarled back, 'And who the hell do you think you are, little lady? Bouvier?' His raucous laughter was echoed by the others.

Moving to rescue her, Kane saw the squaring of her slender shoulders, the dignity with which she lifted her head before answering simply, 'That's exactly who I am.'

Seeing the way that quiet anger drained the colour from the men's faces, Kane felt something wrench in his gut. She was proud of who she was; proud of everything her family had worked for and which she now represented. She had wanted to be part of it, but Ranulph hadn't let her. He had tried to dominate her—as he tried to dominate everyone around him—only she had too much mettle and calibre, despite that vulnerable exterior, to be subjugated by any man. Instead she had found her own way to fulfil her need to be useful—to feel needed. By helping others who needed her.

He was, he realised, seeing a new Shannon. But no, not a new one, he thought self-deprecatingly now. One who had been there all along, only he had been too blinkered by his own prejudices to see her.

The men had slipped off the stools and two of them were attempting to persuade their third and loudest member to leave quietly. The worse for drink, however, he shrugged them off, determined to have the last word.

'So that troubleshooter I saw you with—that...' he gave a little swagger '...*dynamo* they called in to sort the mess out— turn the company around—is he turning you around too?' He started to shake with laughter at his own coarse innuendo, but the next minute the laughter vanished and he and his companions were fleeing out of the exit as fast as rabbits down a dark hole.

Kane was right behind her, and he'd overheard, Shannon realised from his glowering features, which explained the men's sudden scuttling away like that.

'Come on,' he advised gently, taking her elbow, thinking that she looked all in.

Shannon tilted her head, saw the tender concern in his face and overwhelming emotion surged up inside her, a feeling for him that she couldn't have hidden even if she had wanted to. She had never, she thought hopelessly, loved anyone so much in her life.

'Is it true?' she murmured in a small voice as he retrieved her thin silk wrap from the cloakroom attendant and placed it gently around her shoulders. 'Is the company finished?'

'No.'

They were moving across the foyer when a camera suddenly flashed in their faces. Kane looked as though he was about to hit the man who sidestepped with a, 'Thank you, Miss Bouvier,' before shooting off towards the party.

'You're just saying that,' she challenged unhappily, stepping out into the well-lit street. It was late and yet the place was buzzing. The whole world, it seemed, had come to life.

'I've been there for the past ten months,' Kane told her. 'Trust me.' He led her across the busy road, onto the lamplit promenade. It looked so different at night.

'You aren't just one of my father's directors, are you?' she acknowledged. A troubleshooter, the man had said, which meant he called the shots, which also meant that something she'd overheard tonight about Kane rocketing to the top of the business ladder after some clever share dealing was true. And now he was selling his enviable skills—no doubt for a colossal salary—to get the firm he'd walked out of back on its feet.

'No,' he answered and then, confirming it, 'I was called in purely to pull the company out of trouble.'

'For how long?'

'I said I'd stay a year.' So his time with them was nearly up—just as it was with her, she thought achingly, turning her troubled features towards the night-shadowed beach and the restless sea. 'But enough about me,' he said. 'More importantly...' his voice was unbearably gentle '...tell me about Peru.'

So, composing herself after a few moments, she did, from her meeting with Piers and his wife, who had been her flying tutor in Milan—to the disaster-relief work which they'd both been involved in abroad. 'I read an appeal through the charity they supported about floods in Peru wiping out villages, and I wanted to do something really positive to help. When Piers and Jackie flew out there, I went with them. I saw the poverty in some of those places and the conditions people were having to face, and the lack of prospects—particularly for the children—so I stayed on.'

'And you said nothing.' His words were strung with amazement and something else. What was it? she wondered yearningly. Respect?

She shrugged, and all she said was, 'There didn't seem to be much point.'

The moon wasn't quite so full as it had been three nights ago, she noticed as they came onto the quayside. There was a little piece missing, as though someone had snatched at it and broken a bit off.

'It will probably be all over the newspapers tomorrow that we're lovers.' Her voice was thick with longing.

'Do you mind?'

He was asking *her*? 'Not if you don't.'

'It will soon blow over,' he murmured dismissively.

Like the mistral that blew down from the mountains and chilled this region in winter, she thought, suddenly shivering violently.

'Here.'

She caught her breath as he placed his jacket lightly around her shoulders. It was warm from his body heat; smelled of his cologne. To lose herself in both was an almost crucifying ache inside.

The yacht was waiting like a silent predator, gleaming in the moonlight, sleek and powerful, a millionaire's dream.

'It's yours, isn't it?' Shannon said, not needing an answer.

'Yes.'

As she had known—deep down—from the first.

The saloon was in darkness as she stepped down from the patio doors, only the little lights under the aft deck roof guiding their way inside.

Kane was standing on the steps with his back to the closed doors so that she couldn't see his face.

'Thanks for the loan of your jacket.' She let it slide from her shoulders, but was still hanging on to it as she moved over to the settee, hanging on to the scent and texture of all she would ever know of him, because she couldn't break through into this man's heart and make him love her as she loved him. Because they were flying home tomorrow…

'Shannon…'

The sensuality with which he spoke her name immobilised her, holding her there with her back towards him, like an insect in a Venus flytrap, a victim of her fate.

He was still standing by the doors, but with a sixth sense she knew the moment he stepped down into the shadows, knew every measured step he took towards her, the exact second before his fingers lightly brushed her arm in a silent, sensual command.

Her heart seemed to stop beating, and only the drugging power of his will had her turning round to face him. Then she was aware only of being in his arms and of him kissing her, hungrily—passionately—as though there were no barriers between them; as though he would never stop.

CHAPTER NINE

PRESSED against the electrifying length of his body, Shannon clung to him as if he were the only tangible thing left in the universe, alive only to his hard warmth through the fine silk shirt and that firm, insistent mouth devouring her.

They were both breathless when he pulled back and lifted his head to look at her.

This is it, she thought despairingly. This is where he tells me that I've got what I deserve and to go to bed. Dear heaven! *She couldn't bear it!*

Her eyes were dark with need and in the shadows she couldn't see what was in his—didn't want to recognise the mockery she was sure was burning there—and hopelessly she dropped her head against the roughening stubble of his jaw with a little anguished groan.

His hands—warm over her bare back—were suddenly pulling her back against him, his teeth urgently grazing the tender skin of her throat, making her cry out in unashamed need. 'Oh, Kane, don't leave me! Please love me!'

She felt the tension that racked his body, heard his harshly drawn breath shudder through his lungs. Gently then, he took her hand and she obeyed the briefest gesture he made towards the aperture at the aft end of the saloon, preceding him through it with her heart racing, down the curving, carpeted stairs into the master suite.

She had never been down into this part of the yacht before. Aside from the engine room, the aft stateroom was separated by a wall from the other cabins, and was entirely self-contained.

Two lamps were burning dimly on either side of the magnificent double bed, set in an ambience of unashamed luxury. It was all sensuous curves and black lacquered wood, from the rounded bed with its heavy gold counterpane and sumptuous black and gold cushions, to the sweeping dressing table and the dark-framed circular mirror that filled most of the ceiling, providing an even greater illusion of space.

She turned around and saw Kane standing there behind her.

'It's big,' she murmured in a trembling whisper.

His mouth curved with wry sensuality. 'Yes.'

And she would know! she thought, tense with longing, drowning in her emotion. Or was it his? She couldn't tell any more.

She wasn't sure who moved first, but she was in his arms again, he was kissing her and she was kissing him back, their mouths melding with a desperation bordering on the insane.

'Shannon…' Her name was dragged from deep in his throat and she felt the trembling in his body before he lifted her up to carry her the short distance to the bed.

With undisguised urgency he tossed the cushions aside. Then his mouth was over hers, pressing her down into the pillows, the crushing weight of his body as he lowered himself onto her awakening all her responses into vibrant, throbbing life; to the thrilling awareness of his hard arousal.

'You drive me mad,' he groaned on a harshly drawn breath. 'You've always driven me mad!' And she couldn't tell whether he was angry or not because of the passions that rode him, rode them both. Nor did she want to think about that because he was tugging at her dress, pulling the flimsy fabric back to expose her soft breasts and claim the sensitive tip of one with his warm mouth.

She arched against him, wanting more—more than she had ever wanted in her life, his blend of tenderness and passion, as his lips and hands caressed her, dragging little guttural sobs from her throat.

The cabin was soundproofed—made for loving. It was an abstracted recognition rather than pure thought.

Softly her eyes flickered open to the pale suede ceiling, falling on the huge mirror that reflected them both lying there on the bed. She gave a small, shocked gasp, seeing herself, hair loose and wild and totally naked, wondering by what miracle he had managed to dispense with her clothes while, but for his gaping shirt—which her urgent fingers had torn open—he remained fully dressed himself.

With a drugged fascination she watched that bronzed hand caress the golden length of her thigh, the dark masculine head dip in exquisite attention to her breast. Then he stirred, saw where her shocked, absorbed interest lay, and he gave her a rather wry smile in return.

'Voyeurism, darling? Do you like watching what I do to you?'

'No,' she murmured, closing her eyes. But she did, she thought, afraid to tell him, afraid what he would think of her if she said that whatever he did to her she wanted to absorb through all her faculties, only now she kept her eyes closed, wanting only sensation, the ecstasy of his touch.

'For what it's worth,' he murmured with his lips against her hair, 'I don't go in for visual performances every time I make love.'

'I know.' She didn't know how she knew, only that he was too sophisticated a lover to need any props to enhance his own or his partner's pleasure. Briefly then she thought of the other women who must have walked through his life—tried not to think about those who still would—that she was just another player on the stage of his glorious experience.

'Kane...' As she watched him pull off his shirt, reach for the dark band around his waist, a little knot of tension tightened inside her. Should she tell him? 'Kane, I...'

'Hush,' he murmured against her mouth, before he lowered himself onto her, muscular and big and beautiful. She had never thought of a man as beautiful before, but he was, she thought, gasping from the incredibly arousing warmth of his nakedness. 'Do you think I haven't wanted you?' So he had misinterpreted the reason for her tense little utterance, she realised, even as he shuddered with his need of her. 'You'll never know how much.' But he proceeded to show her, using his mouth and hands and voice to bring her back to such a pinnacle of wanting that she couldn't think of anything—do anything—but sob her need for him to take her.

And when he did there was excitement and sudden sharp pain that made her cry out, causing him to hesitate with shocked realisation, but it was already too late. He groaned deeply in his throat as he started to move again, despairing at his overwhelming need of her—his hopeless loss of control. But the sounds torn from her now were only of ecstasy as he continued pushing through, taking her with him through the boundaries of unbelievable pleasure until the mutual throbbing climax that caused silent tears to stream down Shannon's cheeks, and she thought, *This is my universe! This is where I belong!*

She was lying on her back, with her legs drawn up to one side, after he disentangled himself from her, but as though reluctant to see herself in the mirror, or face his hard scrutiny, she turned away, her tension apparent as she waited for the barrage of questions she knew would come.

'Tell me I didn't just imagine that,' he breathed, though he didn't need to ask. That small bloodstain on the coverlet was proof enough. 'Shannon?' She was lying on her side, curled into a tight ball as though to protect herself from an exposure that went far deeper, he sensed, than just the physical. 'Tell me I didn't just make love to a virgin,' he pressed quietly.

'Why?' She sounded small and lost, but she did half turn to face him, and there was a sudden hint of the old teasing in her eyes and her wan smile as she said, 'Am I your first?'

'Yes.' He shook his head, his dishevelled hair falling loosely over his forehead. 'I don't know.' How the hell would he know? 'As far as I'm aware. But what matters is that I was yours.'

'Why?' A line deepened between her brows, and the teasing went out of her eyes—dark underneath from her mascara—smudged like her lipstick from the driving demands of mutual passion. 'Why does it matter?'

He shook his head again. 'It doesn't,' he consoled her. 'It's just that I thought you were...'

'Experienced? Is that why you made love to me without using anything? Because you thought I was taking care of myself?'

It wasn't an accusation, just a statement of fact. Nevertheless he chided himself for his behaviour. If he had thought that, then he would have been wrong to assume—to neglect responsibility, he thought. He never had before, only never had he felt quite like this before...

'No.' Contrition marked the sort of half-smile he gave her. 'But your affair with Markham...'

'We didn't have an affair,' she murmured, looking up into those perplexed, breathtakingly handsome features. 'Well, not like you think. I met him at one of the many parties that seemed to swamp my life at the time—that everyone seemed hell-bent on inviting me to. I think they were a way out—a means of getting myself noticed to replace the attention, the respect I wasn't getting from the people who mattered to me. My friends—or the people I thought were my friends,' she amended with a grimace. 'My father. You.'

A frown knitted Kane's brows as his eyes searched the soft, guileless honesty of her face.

'I knew he was married,' she went on, before he could comment, 'but he told me he was in the process of a very tricky divorce. He was nice to talk to and he seemed interested in the things I believed in. The things I wanted to do.'

'Like save the world?'

'Like trying to make life easier—even possible—for people who weren't born nearly as privileged as I was,' she stressed in response to that indulgent little chuckle in his voice. 'And he pursued me with a vengeance.' She let out a shuddering breath as she remembered it now. 'I didn't want to get involved with him until his divorce was finalised. He said it was only a matter of weeks but that perhaps it was best that we weren't seen together publicly anyway until then to protect me. Protect *me!*' The small laugh that escaped her held anything but mirth. 'Things were getting intolerable at home and when he suggested we go away for the summer together it seemed so idyllic, but I told him I wouldn't sleep with him— not until he was legally free. I surprised myself with how easy it was not to share his bed. I thought that there was something wrong with me because I didn't feel as turned on by him as I knew it was possible to be by—someone, but I told myself that that wasn't important, that it was our intellectual rapport and our friendship that counted above everything else. I supposed it was frustration on his part when he started telling me I wasn't normal. I thought maybe I wasn't—that he really was concerned about me and was trying to help me when he kept insisting I tell him if I'd ever had that kind of feeling for anyone else. So one day I told him.'

'Told him what?' In the stillness of the cabin, Kane's voice was quietly probing.

Closing her eyes, breath held, Shannon hesitated, then in a shuddering whisper said, 'That I wasn't completely abnormal because I used to get turned on thinking about you.' There— it was out. She had said it. And it didn't matter now what he thought about her, because he knew. 'After that he started trying to arouse me...using you as...' Shame choking her, she turned swiftly away from him, adopting the same defensive position, every vertebra thrown into relief along the slender curvature of her spine. Because, of course, when he had seen the distress it caused her he had laughed in her face, telling her he could do without what Kane Falconer hadn't wanted. 'I decided he was sick—that he just wanted to hurt me—and I knew I had to end our relationship. I planned to tell him that weekend, after I'd sorted out somewhere else to go. I didn't realise that his wife had found out about us—that he wasn't even getting a divorce. But then that story broke about her taking an overdose.'

'And you didn't even try to defend yourself?'

'I was scared,' she admitted, her body rigid from the memory. 'I was frightened that if I told the papers he was lying about us being lovers, dented his ego—and he had one hell of an ego to dent—he'd tell everyone what I'd told him. That he'd splash your name across the papers, and you...'

'Wouldn't be flattered that the most desirable girl in London only wanted to make love with me?'

She closed her eyes tight against the stark reality of his words, feeling the shame she would have felt had that been printed; the raw agony of his angry knowledge of it.

'So it's all been an act? One big performance for the gossip columnists?' He couldn't entirely hide his shocked amazement, or the purely masculine elation he was suddenly feeling.

'It was what they expected of me,' she said bitterly, still coiled towards the window. 'The more they tried to slate me, the more determined I was to stay self-contained—whole—intact. None of the men I dated, though, would ever admit to that.' That grievous little note still penetrated her words.

'Shannon...' The hand drawing her back to him was surprisingly gentle. 'So you're saying that all these years you've been keeping yourself for me?'

'No,' she tried to deny, because how insane was that? But he laughed softly, not as Jason had, not with any malice, just with a gentle, sensual rejection of her denial.

'I'm very glad you did.' He leaned across her and with unbearable tenderness kissed the sensitive flesh above the soft curve of her hip, before his fingers splayed out, moving over her with possessive, unbelievable skill.

With cultivated ease he was arousing her again and she groaned beneath his pleasuring hands, her body unfolding for him in unconditional surrender. He wouldn't hurt her as Jason, as other men had—not intentionally anyway. Only when he broke her heart when he decided to move on. But for now that didn't matter. All that mattered was that she had opened her mind, heart and body to this one man and that she was his, forever—or for however long he dictated she should remain so.

Lying in the darkness under the covers, Kane dragged himself back from the warm, sweet aftermath of lovemaking.

Shannon was still sleeping, damp and slick, beside him. He could feel her breasts lifting just above his arm that was still curled around her, and he felt his body responding again to the warm contact of her silky thigh, trapped beneath the possessive strength of his.

She had given him everything—every last ounce of herself, he realised—with her lovemaking, and that staggering admission that he still couldn't quite make himself believe. That when he had watched her from a distance blossoming into a beautiful young woman, resenting every man with whom she was apparently involved, she had wanted him—wanted none of them except him. And he had been oblivious to it, staying aloof from her as a way of dealing with the way he felt, while she had used her beauty and her sensuality to feign a lifestyle that had only strengthened that spurious reputation she had created for herself, rather than let anyone see the real Shannon Bouvier—rather than let him know.

Desire burned in his loins like an incurable fever, a throb of need that only the moist warmth of her femininity could assuage.

Raising himself up, gently he kissed the pale gold of her

hairline and the small dark bruise just above her temple. She smelled of Amarige, musky with loving.

She stirred, giving a small groan, but it was the soft sound of desire because even in her semi-consciousness she was reaching for him, her hands sliding along his back, her mouth warm and willing beneath his.

How many times had he loved her tonight since he had brought her back here from the hotel? Two? Three? He had lost count, and still he couldn't get enough of her. Already he was fully aroused and ready to take her. There was no need for any foreplay on either side.

When his thighs nudged hers apart, she moved eagerly to accommodate him, gasping from the ecstasy of his entering her. And then sensation was overwhelming them both again, and this time was as the last had been—even more intense than the time before, so that she gripped him hard while the power of his body poured into hers until he collapsed heavily on top of her and the spasms of their shattering orgasm ebbed away.

Some time later, while she still lay beneath him, and his lips were idly caressing her throat, he breathed hoarsely, 'Marry me.'

'What?'

He reached up, switching on one of the lamps above the bed. She looked surprised, he noticed when their eyes had adjusted, almost as surprised as he felt himself. He had never proposed to anyone before—though he had come close to it once a few years ago—and hadn't anticipated that he would be doing so now, because he was hardly what one could call the impetuous type. He only knew, though, that he could never bear to think of Shannon in another man's arms again. Even watching her talking to other men tonight had driven him nearly insane with jealousy and she was far too lovely—and much too good a catch, he thought drily—to leave loose out there in the big wide world. He couldn't—wouldn't—risk losing her affections to another man. Not now. Not after this.

'I want you to be my wife,' he rephrased, thinking that that sounded less like begging.

She gave a disbelieving little laugh, a small, bewildered shake of her head. 'Are you really asking me?'

'Do I have to put it in writing?'

'No…I mean…why?' she breathed, her expression incredulous.

'Why?' He fished around for a reason that wouldn't make him sound like a smitten adolescent. 'OK. I'm not very good at this. But what about because you drive me crazy? Because I don't think I'll ever sleep again if you aren't there beside me. Because if we carry on like this you're going to get pregnant—and because it's time someone took you out of circulation and put an end to all those rumours and that charade you've cultivated for all those years, and because I can't think of anybody better—or more qualified—' he smiled as caressing fingers over her breast made her eyes close with desire '—than I am to do it.'

'Is that all?' She laughed again, but it was with immeasurable relief to Kane to realise it was with joy this time.

'You really mean it, don't you?' Tears were making her eyes glisten like sapphires. 'But I…' Smiling, bewildered, she was shaking her head. 'I thought you didn't even *like* me!'

'Not like you?' His mouth compressed at his own futile struggle to convince himself of that. 'I wanted to kill every man who ever dared to touch you. Kiss you…' His lips lightly brushing hers staked their own claim now.

'But until yesterday I thought you were involved with someone…' She couldn't forget the anguish of imagining him with another woman, the joy and relief in finding out that she had been wrong. 'Why did you let me think that?'

Gently he traced a path from the hollow of her throat to the silken valley of her breasts with his index finger. 'Because knowing you thought I had a lover and laying claim to one was the only way I knew of keeping my hands off you.'

She bit her lower lip provocatively, delighting in holding sway over such a strong, dynamic man. 'And will I get to meet this sister of yours?' she queried lightly.

'Only if you marry me. Well?' he prompted, looking suddenly just a little bit unsure.

'Oh, Kane! Of course I'll marry you!' She sat up, flinging her arms around his neck. 'Did you think I wouldn't?' She pulled back a little to look at him, drawing a hand down the hard line of his cheek, the grazing stubble of his jaw, her fingers moving sensuously across his mouth.

'No.'

'You're arrogant!' she teased, and saw his mouth pull in wry acknowledgement.

'One of my few faults,' he accepted

'Modest, too!' Laughing still, she was flopping back against the pillows, spreading her arms wide as though she were embracing the whole universe. 'Mrs Kane Falconer.'

'Sounds good,' he murmured, gazing down on her rapt face and her soft, enticing nakedness with a satisfied firming of his mouth.

'Mrs *Shannon* Falconer,' she amended with a teasing smile, trying it out.

'Say it any way you like,' he breathed, before he claimed the sweetness of her lovely mouth. 'The outcome's still the same.'

Which was Shannon Bouvier—exactly where she belonged, he thought with a swelling satisfaction. With him. In his life. In his bed.

The fact that he was doing exactly what Ranulph Bouvier wanted struck him with staggering clarity suddenly, although it seemed to be of such little consequence now. Even so, now that Shannon would be permanently in his care, that couldn't, he realised, fail to please his future father-in-law. As for himself, he would have everything he wanted, he thought with a surge of hot, possessive pride. Everything he had wanted all along...

The sun was shining as they touched down in London and walked out of the busy airport terminal to Kane's waiting car.

Delivered for him as previously arranged, it was a dark Mercedes convertible, big and sleek and powerful. Like its owner, Shannon couldn't help thinking with her heart overflowing, as he stowed their luggage, with the small holdall containing the few clothes his sister had left on board, away in the boot.

Now, as they were weaving expertly in and out of the surging traffic, Kane sent a glance across the pale cream interior. 'Are you nervous?'

He meant about seeing her father and she simply nodded. From the moment they had touched down, her stomach had been twisted in knots.

'Don't be,' he said, his voice quietly reassuring over the purr of the engine. 'I'll break the news to him that you're back if you want to go home first. Or you can come and face him in the office with me.'

She thought of the big, empty house that she had fled so unhappily over two and a half years ago. She didn't want to go back there and wait for the rest of the day wondering how her father would receive her; what lectures she might have to endure before he allowed her to feel that she was accepted back again.

'I'll come to the office. But I'll see him on my own,' she told Kane determinedly. 'He's my father and—'

The sudden trill of the phone ringing in its cradle interrupted her. Automatically Kane touched a button to take the call.

'Hello, Kane. Where are you?' It was the rather plummy voice of Ranulph's secretary coming over the speaker.

'I'm back in London. I should be with you in…' Tilting a hand on the wheel, consulting his watch, he gave her a rough estimation.

'Are you alone?'

'No,' he said, and after the briefest pause, 'In the strictest confidence, I've got Shannon with me. Whatever you need to say, you can go ahead.'

There was a moment's silence when Shannon wondered if they had been cut off. Then the voice returned, sounding clipped and confidential. 'Can you ring me back?'

Whatever it was, the woman wanted only Kane to hear it, Shannon realised, the glow she was feeling inside today tarnished a little from the knowledge that she was still regarded as superfluous to what was going on, so that when he found a suitable lay-by to pull over and pick up the phone, she reached for the door handle, suggesting with mock carelessness, 'Perhaps I should get out.'

A hand caught her arm, detaining her even as he spoke into the mouthpiece.

'What?' Silence. 'When?' The grip on her arm tightened. 'How bad is it?' he was demanding, this last question bringing Shannon's head round, her gaze riveted on his face.

'What is it?' she whispered, seeing the deepening lines around his mouth and jaw. 'What's wrong?'

'It's your father. He's had a heart attack. They've rushed him to the hospital.'

'Is it bad?'

'Yes,' he said, wishing there was a way he could break it to her gently, yet knowing instinctively that this girl who saved the world's children and challenged drunks in the name of family honour would want nothing but the truth. 'It looks very bad.'

CHAPTER TEN

THE hands clamped over Shannon's eyes smelled of a tangy and unmistakable aftershave lotion.

'I want to take you to bed,' Kane whispered from behind, his breath fanning the strands of blonde hair that weren't caught up in the elegant French pleat.

It was the first time since that day, over three weeks ago, that he had shown any real playfulness towards her; that dreadful day when they had returned from France to learn that Ranulph Bouvier was not only very ill, but also not expected to recover.

'Someone might come in!' Shannon laughed tremulously, pulling away from the masculine hand that slid inside her jacket to massage her instantly responsive breast. Not only was the boardroom door open, but anyone could pass at any time.

'Coming from a girl who likes mirrors on the ceiling and enticing me in white leather, I find your modesty charming,' he grinned, moving over and turning the *Meeting in Progress* sign round on the door, before closing it with a purpose Shannon knew would send a ripple through the adjoining office.

'People will guess,' she breathed in mock objection because it had been such a traumatic time they hadn't made their engagement public yet. Nevertheless she couldn't hide the feverish glitter in her eyes.

'Don't you think they already know?'

Yes, she thought with colour stealing up into her cheeks, but not from any obvious display of his carnal knowledge of her. Just with the subtle softening of his voice when he spoke to her sometimes; in a clash of glances; in the occasional proprietary touch of his hand on her arm.

It was clear from the beginning that everyone at Bouvier Developments held Kane in the greatest esteem, from the highest level of management to the most junior clerks. In less than a year he had turned the company's fortunes around and helped re-establish the firm as a healthy rival among its competitors, and without Ranulph to oppose him he had insisted that Shannon join his team for managerial training and get herself fully involved.

Just being at his side, she realised, had earned her their respect. But gradually they were beginning to respect her in her own right, appreciate her capabilities and her burgeoning business sense; accept her as a valuable asset and not merely to humour her just because of who she was.

Now, as she slid into Kane's arms, felt his hungry mouth on hers and his hands moving over the black tailored trouser suit that hugged her slender body, she groaned her appreciation of all he meant to her, of the evidence of his potent need of her through the fine, dark cloth of his suit.

'I want to announce our engagement—and soon,' he breathed huskily, sounding impatient. 'I want you to move in with me—not just snatch a few odd moments or hours together before one of us has to leave.' He had suggested it in the beginning, but with her father in a coma and hospitalised she hadn't felt the time was right to move into his apartment. Besides, there had been far too much to take care of back at the house.

'I can't wait for you much longer,' he murmured, before lifting her up onto the long, glossy table where multimillion-pound deals were struck, but where they fell back together now in almost mutual desperation for each other. It had been nearly four weeks since that night of endless passion on the boat, and since they had been able to fully relax together. There had been too much to worry about. Too much to do…

Now though, as his mouth moved over her throat and his hand slipped beneath the powder-blue silk covering her breast, she moaned her assent, powerless to do anything but surrender.

'I don't think making love on a table is what I want to do with you. At least, not this table anyway,' he chuckled softly against her mouth, drawing back just as the intercom buzzed right beside them.

'Just to remind you…you've got another meeting, Kane,' Ranulph's secretary's voice informed him with her usual cool efficiency. 'In fifteen minutes. And I've got Chesterton's on the phone.' There was a significant pause. 'They want to speak to Shannon.'

Shannon sat up quickly, pulling her blouse together. 'OK. I'll take it—in my father's office.' She sounded, she knew, as though she'd been doing nothing else but making love with the acting chairman.

'Well done,' Kane murmured, smiling as he switched off the intercom, and she knew he wasn't talking about her efforts to try and conceal what they had been doing. 'I've trained you well if our biggest customer insists only on speaking to a Bouvier.'

'No, you've given me much more than that, Kane,' she whispered, slipping off the table. He'd given her a chance; some status in the company. Respect.

She recalled how excluded she had felt when her father's PA had rung that day when they had been on their way home from the airport and had wanted to speak to him privately, as though she, Shannon, were an outsider, and not the heiress to the Bouvier millions! But the woman, it dawned on Shannon later, had probably only wanted to spare her the trauma of hearing what she needed to know over the phone. Or perhaps she'd simply thought Kane would be more equipped—as he had been—to break the news to her that her father might not survive.

'We'll make him proud of you,' he breathed, opening the door for her, seeming, as he always did, to read her thoughts. Because, against all the odds, Ranulph Bouvier had surprised everyone, coming off his ventilator after a long worrying spell to boom orders at the nurses from the aggravating confines of his bed.

'They told me you were here,' he had said when he had woken up from a natural and restful sleep and seen Shannon sitting there, with only a kind of relieved acceptance on his flaccid and rather ruddy face. Absently he had patted the slim hand resting on his bed, as though she were some rather tiresome pet to whom he was obliged to show affection. 'I'm glad at any rate Kane made you see sense about coming home. You always did show respect for him—if not for me.'

Because he respects me in turn—recognises my worth as a human being! Shannon had ached to say, but didn't. She didn't want to upset her father, or do anything that would hinder his progress in making a good—if not full—recovery. He would have to take things more easily, the doctors had told him without pulling any punches—if he valued his life. And then suddenly, the previous evening, during her usual visiting time, she had learned that he was expected out of hospital very soon.

If she had been hoping that a chance to look after him while he was convalescing might help some bond to grow between them, then he had waved that hope aside by telling her he didn't need her fussing around; that he was engaging a private nurse to do that.

'Kane tells me you've been at the office—that you're a valuable addition.' He'd grimaced as though he hadn't wholly believed it. 'You stay and help out. I'm sure you'll be useful.'

Useful, she had thought. Not essential or very necessary. But *useful*.

At least that was something, she decided now with tears glistening in her eyes as she crossed his office to take the call.

Perhaps in another hundred years he might even consider her capable of having some say! But what did it matter anyway? she thought, smiling through her tears. Just as long as she had Kane's love.

The next few days seemed to pass in a whirl of excitement for Shannon, when Kane made their engagement public after slipping the diamond-clustered sapphire she had chosen on her finger.

There was dealing with the Press and their probing questions, all of which Kane dismissed with polite but enviable succinctness. And there was meeting the academic young woman who breezed into the office one morning, insisting that Kane take both her and his new fiancée to lunch.

'You didn't lose him to Emily Coltrane, then,' Sophie Falconer teased when, after eating, they were sitting alone together in the intimate little bistro while Kane settled the bill at the bar. Her smile was subtle, like the lift of her eyebrow beneath her dark, heavily fringed, trendy hair. Like her brother, Shannon thought, this nineteen-year-old needed to say very little to get her point across.

Wondering if anyone in the restaurant was as happy as she was at that moment, she responded with a wry smile and said, 'It was touch and go.'

Both girls laughed, with Shannon reinforcing the view she had formed almost immediately on meeting her future sister-in-law—that she liked her, very much.

Tanned from a month in Spain that concluded her gap year between leaving college and entering one of the country's most prestigious universities, Sophie Falconer was mature, independent and knew exactly where she was going in life. It was also obvious from the occasional fond glance she sent towards the tall, dynamic-looking man standing at the bar that she adored her brother.

'I understand he kidnapped you—and that you were forced

to borrow my clothes!' Sophie glanced upwards at Kane, who was just returning to their table. 'I never thought you had it in you, brother dear!'

'I thought I explained. Only because she wasn't well,' Kane emphasised, leaning on his chair and directing a look at Shannon that made her stomach do a strange little somersault.

'But then he kitted me out in St Tropez,' she joined in, realising there would be very few secrets between this brother and sister.

'St Tropez?' Sophie tilted her head back and grinned up at him. 'He does, of course, take the most discerning of his women there,' she commented, her tongue curled mischievously to one side, then ducked to avoid a mock cuff around the head from one immaculate, dark-sleeved arm.

'And that's the last time one young woman will be going there,' he promised playfully, the smile he exchanged with Shannon sending a river of warmth through her blood.

He was everything she had ever imagined he would be, she thought, her heart swelling with love for him. Warm. Caring. Generous. Because of course, when she had sold some of her jewellery to pay back the cost of the clothes and accessories he had bought for her during that trip, he had insisted that she put the money into her foundation, a charitable trust he had helped her set up in her own name since coming home to aid the underprivileged and needy children with whom she had worked.

'You must have knocked him for six,' Sophie commented in an amazed whisper, wise to that intimate exchange between Shannon and her brother. 'Only a few months ago he was swearing allegiance to lifelong bachelordom!'

'Don't listen to her,' Kane drawled, pulling out her chair as she stood up.

'Why not?' Shannon laughed over her shoulder, but she was only teasing. It might all have happened as fast as Sophie had implied, she thought, almost giddy with emotion, but she had never felt so sure of anything—or so happy—in her life.

At first, Ranulph Bouvier had expressed only mild surprise when Shannon happily flashed the ring before him at his hospital bedside and told him of her future plans.

'Congratulations,' he had said, and that was all, although beneath his inexorable features she did think that he looked secretly pleased.

Later that week, the hospital discharged him, and Shannon took the day off to prepare for his homecoming.

'I don't know why you wanted to concern yourself with company matters,' he said plainly when the nurse he had hired was settling in to her suite of rooms and he and Shannon were alone together for the first time in the imposing drawing room. 'I thought I was bringing you up to be a support to a successful husband. It was enough for your mother.' She was tucking a blanket around him where he sat in his tartan dressing gown in his favourite chair beside the impressive Regency fireplace. This house was too big and too unwelcoming, she thought, but it didn't intimidate her—he didn't intimidate her any more.

'No, it wasn't,' she contradicted quietly, firmly. 'She wanted to be a proficient showjumper. Go in for all the trials. Train for the Olympics. But she shelved her dreams to be everything her husband wanted,' she reminded him of the self-sacrificing, gentle mother she remembered. 'I'm not so compliant. I'm much more like you.'

'Hmm,' he snorted, grimacing, but there was a surprising flash of something almost like approval in his watery grey eyes. 'Well, let's hope Kane can curb that.'

And he just had to tag that on, Shannon felt, refusing to let anything spoil her happiness as he caught the hand that was tucking him in, ran his thumb over the clustered sapphire that glistened there. 'You've obviously got what you want, and so has he.'

'I hope so,' she smiled, her face glowing.

'I think most definitely,' he said, releasing her to pick up the glass of orange juice on the table beside him, which the nurse had insisted he drink instead of his usual hot toddy. 'And so will I when you eventually give me an heir. At least you've picked the right man for the job.' He pulled a face at the glass he was setting back down on the table. 'He's the right man all round—for both of us, Shannon. With his vested interest in the shareholding he has, which he bought when prices were at rock-bottom, I knew he'd work wonders for us if I persuaded him to come back. He knows what he can expect for bringing you home and has done for months— nothing less than the ultimate premium as soon as he marries you.'

A sudden little shiver ran down Shannon's spine. 'And what's that?' she queried, looking askance at him.

'The controlling interest in the company.'

'Controlling...' A line deepened between her eyes, her voice tailing away.

'Oh, he professed not to want it in the beginning—refused the whole package I was offering,' Ranulph went on, oblivious to the pain suddenly darkening her eyes.

'Package?' she echoed, feeling an inexplicable chill spreading through her. 'So...you sent him off in his yacht and...he came looking for me?' she asked wretchedly. Like a marauding buccaneer—out to claim his bounty. Dear heaven! She couldn't believe that about Kane. Not the man she loved! She couldn't!

'His yacht?' Ranulph was frowning up at her. 'Did he bring you back on a yacht? Is that how he wooed you?' From the broadening smile that spread across his face, he looked remarkably impressed. 'When he said he met up with you in Barcelona, I thought you'd flown back. I've got to hand it to him—he's as proficient in handling women as he is in kick-starting underperforming companies. That man's know-how is second to none. He's built up a flourishing enterprise of his own in the few years he's been away, and—though I shouldn't say it—he doesn't need us any more. Walking out on us at the time he did was the turning point of his life. A few clever moves in the right direction and—hey presto! The man's a multimillionaire! But now he's making the best move of all—as I'm sure he's aware—in marrying you.'

No! Swiftly—emphatically—she said, 'It's because he *loves* me!'

'Possibly.' Ranulph's mouth compressed. 'But I don't want any daughter of mine going into marriage blindfolded. It's up to a woman to keep the love nest warm. Men like Kane aren't driven by sentiment.'

'What, then? If he's so rich? Why's he so keen to get even richer?'

'You've got to understand, girl…understand it as your mother did…' now, as a flaccid chin came to rest on the pyramid of his hands, she saw something akin to sympathy in her father's eyes '…it isn't about making money. Men like me, like Kane, enjoy the cut and thrust of competition—the power, Shannon. It's like an aphrodisiac. A drug.'

And he was getting more addicted every time he made love to her! she thought, biting back bitter tears. Because she was the key to the even greater fix he craved!

She couldn't believe it. She couldn't! Kane loved her, and he would have told her if her father had suggested a proposal like that.

Or would he? Cruelly, the doubts intensified, hurting, torturing her. He had, after all, been so keen to bring her back home. And he hadn't actually told her he loved her, had he? Oh, he had said so many things! Such as she drove him crazy. And he'd never sleep again without her. But that was a hell of a good way of actually avoiding saying *I love you*, wasn't it?

Telling herself that she should be ashamed of even questioning Kane's feelings towards her, she reminded herself of how tender he was; that no one could pretend to care to such a degree if their only motive was to satisfy a thirst for power.

Well, there was only one way to find out, she realised, pulled between the griping pains of doubt and the aching certainty of his loving her. She'd just have to ask him outright!

She didn't see him that night. Aside from choosing to stay in and keep an eye on Ranulph, she knew that Kane was attending a late meeting in town. It wasn't until the following morning, therefore, that she had the chance to speak to him and then she had to chase all over the modern building to find him before their receptionist told her he had gone into the boardroom earlier, and wasn't taking any calls.

He was standing alone by the long table, sorting out some papers from his briefcase, exuding the wow factor in a light grey suit that accentuated even as it tamed the lean, hard fitness of his body.

'Good morning', he had been about to say, but stopped short as Shannon closed the door quietly behind her. 'What's wrong?' he asked with razor-sharp perception. She looked pale and tense, and there were bluish smudges beneath her eyes.

'Is it true?' she whispered, unusually cool in her lightweight pale blue jacket and trousers. The day was overcast and the draught from an open window was making it chilly in the long room.

'Is what true?' he queried, frowning.

Biting the inside of her cheek, Shannon transferred her gaze to the vase of white lilies in the centre of the highly polished table. 'Has my father offered you the controlling interest in this company?' she asked, bringing her head up at last.

He looked at her obliquely through narrowing eyes. 'What?'

'Has he?' she pressed, her face screwed up with tension.

Calmly he dropped the papers he was holding down onto the table and, rather hesitantly, as though measuring his words, said, 'It has been suggested…yes.'

'In exchange for marrying me?' There, it was out. Her heart racing, she waited for him to deny it.

Eventually he said, 'Did he tell you that?'

'Was it?' Why didn't he deny it? she thought, tortured. Why was he looking so…thrown?

'Well…'

'*Was* it?' Good grief! Why was he hesitating? Why didn't he just laugh and say 'Of course it wasn't'?

'That was his initial proposition—yes,' he answered at length. 'Months ago—but I refused it.'

'But then you changed your mind?'

The eyes raking over her were suddenly coldly assessing, before he said slowly, 'What are you saying?'

Hurting, numb, she murmured, 'So it's true, then.' How could he? 'How could *you*?'

'Shannon, for heaven's sake!' He made a move towards her. She was shaking her head, backing away. 'I thought it was a crazy proposition when he asked me, but I'm sure he was only thinking of you.'

'Of me?' Wounded disbelief flickered in her eyes. 'And you? Were you only thinking of me too? When exactly did you concoct this plot between you?'

'There wasn't any plot!' His answer came back like a whip-lash, but she stood there, meeting his rising anger stride for stride.

'No? What was it? A gentleman's agreement?' Bright wings of colour were spreading along her cheekbones. 'You take my daughter off my hands and bend her to *your* will, and in return I'll give you all the power you want!'

'There isn't any *power*, as you're so dramatically putting it. And you're flattering me and the whole damned male sex if you think any man could bend *you* to his will!' His face was livid and his eyes were blazing. 'Haven't you enough—?'

Angrily he reached for the intercom as it buzzed across their heated conversation, and with cutting *déjà vu*,Shannon recalled the last time they had been alone together in this room. They had wanted each other so badly, they had virtually ravished each other right there and then on the table. His voice had caressed her like silk—as it always did when he made love to her. Not like the cold, incisive tones that were now flaying the young receptionist with nerve-rattling authority. 'I thought I told you—no calls!'

'I only know what my father told me,' Shannon assured him as he cut off the other girl's flustered apology with one angry movement.

'And he had no right to!'

'No, I'll bet he didn't!' she stormed, and now there were bitter tears swimming in her eyes. 'So you set out in your lovely boat and got me on board whether I wanted to come with you or not!'

'Oh, sure I did!'

'And was pretending not to want to seduce me all part of the act? Playing the gallant protector because you knew it was the sure-fire way of getting me to trust you? When all the time I was…' Trying to overturn his invincible self-possession, seduce him; making herself look a fool, never dreaming it was all a carefully constructed plan.

'Is that what you want to believe?' Deep lines were scoring his face as he turned to thrust some papers into his briefcase on the table.

'Wasn't it?' With shaming clarity she remembered how she had called him her father's lackey, ridiculing him for crawling back. She had been stupid not to recognise the extent of his driving ambition, though she had had no idea of exactly how powerful he had become.

'Oh, for heaven's sake, Shannon! What am I supposed to say to a childish statement like that? How many times do I have to tell you? Ranulph suggested it to me—and I refused! All right?'

'So why did you change your mind?'

'I would have thought that was obvious!'

'Why?' she reiterated painfully. *Tell me you love me!* she thought. *Say it—just once!* Only he didn't.

'After all the time we've spent together?' Those steel-cool eyes looked incredulous. 'If you don't know, then I'm afraid I can't tell you.'

Of course not. He wouldn't lie. That much was beneath him.

'What are you imagining?' he asked roughly. 'That I had second thoughts and set out with some devious plan in mind to kidnap you—solely to get you to marry me?'

Her heart ached with wanting to believe that that wasn't the case. But how would she ever know?

'Well, why not?' she flung back at him miserably. And then remembering Ranulph's words about what drove men like Kane, she was adding, 'Why not make the girl fall in love with you first? That was an added bonus, wasn't it?'

'Yes, that could possibly be what clinched it!' His jaw was set in a determined thrust, and his face was flushed with his anger. 'Had I known she had such little faith in me, I might have thought twice before I asked!'

They were shouting at each other, with no side giving any quarter. People would hear their raised voices, Shannon thought, despairing, even if they couldn't make out exactly what was being said.

'If it's just me you want, and not the company, then prove it,' she said wretchedly, knowing even as she said it that a man with his pride would never take up a challenge like that.

'Prove it?' he echoed roughly. 'You have so little trust in me that you ask me to *prove* it?' The sudden heart-stabbing look in his eyes lanced through her more cruelly than anything he might have said. 'If I have to do that,' he snarled as he snapped his briefcase closed and swung it off the table, 'then there's nothing more to be said.'

'Kane!'

The slamming of the boardroom door was all that answered her anguished cry.

CHAPTER ELEVEN

SHANNON didn't know how she got through the next few days. During that first morning, everyone in the office crept around her with a mix of sympathy and awe on their faces. Sympathy in knowing she had been on the receiving end of Kane's formidable temper; awe in realising that she had not only stood up to it, but had easily given back as good as she'd got.

As the day had progressed without a word from him, and then two days slipped painfully into three, then four, Shannon became more and more dispirited.

She'd known that he had had to go away this week. But surely, if he loved her, she kept torturing herself silently, wouldn't he have telephoned to tell her that he understood? That he knew how it must look? That gaining control of the company had been the last thing on his mind when he had asked her to marry him? That he loved her—above everything? That he'd do his best to clear up the whole misunderstanding?

But she had asked him to do that, hadn't she? And that had only resulted in his walking out on her. Or had she been wrong in simply asking for his reassurance?

Sitting in his office, dealing with some of his post that the PA had left for her, Shannon sent a harrowed look towards the telephone beside her, willing it to ring.

She ached to hear his voice. To hear him telling her that he had been wrong to get so angry. That it was an overreaction. That he wanted to see her and couldn't wait to get back to London.

Why? she thought despairingly, dropping her head into her

hands, elbows resting on his huge desk. Why, oh, why wouldn't he ring?

'Shannon?'

She looked up, startled.

'Are you all right?' Stewart Maynard asked. At fifty-two, he was the eldest of the company's directors. A thin and rather indistinct man, his expression behind his rimless glasses was mildly puzzled, concerned.

'I'm fine,' she assured him quickly, not even bothering to feign a headache. What was the point? she thought. Everyone knew she was still feeling the backlash of that dreadful row in the boardroom earlier in the week.

Looking a little awkward and clearly trying to make light of the situation, Stewart remarked, 'You look swallowed up by that chair.'

Meaning it was made for someone who carried more weight—both physically and authoritatively. Someone more commanding. Someone like Kane.

'Well…' Shannon returned, an affected smile concealing how much it hurt to tag on, 'appearances can sometimes be deceiving.'

'Yes, quite.' She knew he had been as surprised as anyone by how effectively she was dealing with her managerial training and the work with her foundation—as though she had been born to it. 'In that case you'll have to keep the new MD in line for us after Kane leaves.'

'Yes…well…that won't be for a few weeks yet, will it?' she reminded him, busying herself with jotting down a note on one of the letters in front of her so that he wouldn't notice how even the mention of Kane's name affected her.

'I…understood,' he said hesitantly, 'that he's decided his job here's complete and that this Channel Island assignment is the last he'll be handling for us personally.' And when she shot an astonished glance up at him, because it was the first she had heard of it, he added, looking decidedly uncomfortable, 'Or so I was led to believe.'

You mean he's leaving early? She wanted to respond with something that would sound as though she knew all about it; not as though he'd made the decision without even telling her. But why had he done it, she wondered, unless he had decided it was over between them? In which case, was all that Ranulph had said about men like Kane only being driven by power true, so that now that his real motives were out in the open did he feel that he couldn't carry on a relationship with her? Marry her? Pretend? Or was he—as she had asked herself endlessly over the past few days, as she so badly wanted to believe—just hurt and angry with her for distrusting him; for having such blatant doubts…?

'Y-yes, of course,' she found herself bluffing now. 'I see.'

'Of course. You knew.' Stewart was trying to make her feel better, she decided. Make her feel as though she weren't the last to know before he went out of the office and told the other directors that the row they had heard coming from that boardroom was probably a lot more serious than they had thought.

Well, it was, wasn't it? she agonised, wishing he would go away and leave her to her misery. Because how much more serious could it be than finding out that the man you loved was only marrying you for his own benefit; and when you challenged him about it, having him walk out on you without even bothering to try and dispute it, without even a call?

Swaying between her love for him and this excruciating suspicion, she had tried to ring him a couple of times, but once his phone had been on voicemail and another time it had been engaged, and after that she had lost her nerve, deciding she'd wait until he came back to speak to him

'What's that?' she asked, dangerously close to tears as Stewart put a file down in front of her.

'It's just some work I've been doing for Chesterton's re-

lating to this Channel Island project. Ranulph was supposed
to be handling it until he was taken ill, which is why Kane
agreed to go over there for him instead. He's leaving
Guernsey tomorrow with the customers and Ranulph's plan
was that I attend the party Kane's putting on for them tomorrow night.'

'In Guernsey?' Shannon frowned, putting her slowness in
following down to an understandable lack of concentration.
'And you want someone to organise a flight for you?'

'No. Kane's bringing them back on the yacht.'

Her heart suddenly started up an irregular rhythm. 'The
yacht?'

'I hear he's got one hell of a super craft…' Stewart was
grinning like a schoolboy '…which he had brought back from
the Med last week, as I'm sure you know.' He paused as
though waiting for her to confirm it. When she didn't, he went
on, 'I was looking forward to the chance of checking it out
myself, but now Ranulph's insisting it should be a Bouvier
who meets them down south tomorrow, so I'm handing it all
over to you.'

No!

'I—I can't possibly,' Shannon stammered, rejecting the
idea outright. How could she go down there to entertain their
biggest customer and face Kane as though nothing had happened? Put on a show of cordiality when her heart felt as
though it were bleeding from so many suspicions? When there
was so much she needed to say to him? To ask? 'I've got far
too much to do here…' She made a hopeless little gesture at
all the paperwork on the desk. 'You really want to go. I think
it's only fair that you should in that case…'

'Ranulph will think it's my doing—going against his decision.' Stewart sounded really worried. 'He knew I was only
too happy to go, but you know what he's like.'

And you won't stand up to him, Shannon thought, remembering from the past that Stewart was one of her father's 'yes' men. *No one will, except Kane. Kane and me.*

Something twisted inside her as she thought how similar they were; how made for each other they had seemed until a few days ago.

But she wanted to see him alone. Not as his hostess at some party he was throwing, though if she raised any objections to Ranulph now, she thought hopelessly, he would only argue and lose his temper. It might even cause a relapse, and she couldn't let that happen. He was making good progress. He had even struck up a rather argumentative but definite rapport with his nurse, who, being middle-aged, could give back as good as he gave, which seemed to be helping him immensely.

No, Shannon decided. She wouldn't do anything to jeopardise his health, no matter how much pain agreeing to his demands caused her.

'All right,' she accepted, defeated, and saw Stewart's shoulders visibly relax. 'I'll go.'

There was tranquillity in the Hampshire countryside after the hectic and congested motorway drive down from London, though it did little to calm the butterflies in Shannon's stomach.

Her pulses were pumping with nervous anticipation as she finally pulled into the marina's car park, far later than she had hoped, and abandoned the black Porsche for the sleek and achingly familiar vessel, already moored there in the mellow evening sun.

As she approached it, her eyes darting over several unfamiliar figures on the flybridge, the soft music and laughter drifting down from its decks assured her that the party had already begun.

Heart racing beneath her simple black dress, Shannon picked out the steps to the aft deck, treading carefully in her high-heeled black sandals, her ears sharpening through the babble of laughter and conversation for the voice she craved to hear.

In a pale cream shirt and light chinos that showed off his lean waist and hips and strong, athletic legs, Kane was standing in the saloon, with his back to the open patio doors, talking to a sophisticated-looking grey-haired couple, whom she guessed were the Chesterton's MD and his wife. There were others, too, milling around. Another couple—slightly younger—as well as the people she'd seen on the upper deck. Other directors, she remembered, whom Stewart had told her were being invited with their partners from Chesterton's head office, which was based in Hampshire, virtually a stone's throw away.

As she came down the steps into the plush interior, someone saw her and touched Kane's arm.

The look on his face, as he turned, registered shock. So no one had told him that she was coming, Shannon despaired, because Stewart had said he would do it.

'Where's Stewart?' he probed quietly, coming up to her, his gaze making her skin prickle with heated awareness as it flitted briefly over her swept-up hair, over the pale gold of her shoulders beneath thin shoelace straps, taking in the alluring side-split of the figure-hugging dress, a dark perplexity the only emotion he was allowing to show.

'My father changed his mind. He wanted me to come in his place.' Dragging her eyes from the tanned flesh of his throat beneath his casually fastened shirt, desperately she searched his face for some recognition of relief. Pleasure. Anything that would tell her that he was more than glad that she had come! But his smile was cool and fleeting and, convinced that he didn't want her there—dreading he would think the whole thing had been her idea, keeping her voice low, quickly she tagged on, 'I didn't arrange it. But I couldn't argue with him—not when he's been so ill.'

'No,' he agreed quietly, his tone impassive, emotionless,

although she had a feeling he was weighing up her every reaction.

She couldn't bear it! Not when she was aching for him to take her in his arms, tell her he had been wrong to storm out of the office as he had; tell her how much he had missed her.

But he didn't, and of course he couldn't with a crowd of people on board, she reasoned, steeling herself against his cool, impersonal facade as he said, 'In that case, we'd better get you a drink. Introduce you properly.' The touch of his hand against her spine was lightly formal, but the burn of his fingers on her bare flesh was almost more than she could cope with at that moment.

In a daze, she heard him make the introductions; heard responses from people to whom, until now, she had only spoken over the telephone.

'I'm sorry to hear about your father.' It was commiserations from the MD's wife as Shannon sipped the tomato juice she had requested from the waiter, while someone else said, 'I do believe congratulations are in order.'

Kane hadn't introduced her as his fiancée, only as the Bouvier representing the company—and hectically she wondered whether she should read anything into that. But now with her heart screaming from her need for reassurance she smiled and made what she was sure was some fatuous comment in return.

'It's a beautiful evening,' Kane suggested. 'Why don't we go outside?'

So somehow she found herself on deck, making conversation with one guest after another. And all the while the music throbbed quietly from hidden speakers, the caterers who had been engaged handed round the finger buffet, and Shannon plastered a smile on her lips and entertained until her face ached, only fully alive to Kane's devastating presence, to the rich timbre of his voice and his deep laughter coming from just behind her, above her on the flybridge, from the saloon as he changed a CD on the music system.

Left alone aft temporarily when the woman to whom she had been talking went inside for her jacket, Shannon felt the hairs rise on the back of her neck and turned from watching the sun setting on the water to meet Kane's far too direct gaze.

'Enjoying yourself?' His tone was coolly mocking.

Feeling herself melting under his probing scrutiny, she sent a glance towards the open doors to the saloon, where some guests had chosen to remain, saying as carelessly as she could, 'You didn't tell me you were leaving.'

His face was a mask of composure. 'I only made the final decision at the weekend. I hadn't had time to tell you.'

'So you humiliated me by letting me find out from Stewart.' Her voice wobbled so she had to fight to hold it steady, to control the hurt as she challenged, 'How do you think that looked?'

'Like we're not speaking,' he supplied flippantly, and then suddenly, without warning, 'To hell with how it looked!' The composure was gone—if it had been there at all—and he seemed to check himself for a moment before going on to say in more conciliatory tones, 'I wasn't trying to humiliate you, Shannon, though you seem hell-bent on believing that that's my only goal in life. A problem's arisen in my own company that needs my time and input more than Bouvier's does now. But Bouvier's will continue to prosper under the new MD with the fresh policies I've put in place. Neither you nor Ranulph need worry yourselves unduly there.'

It all sounded so final. Was that how he meant it to sound? she wondered numbly, as a burst of laughter broke through her misery from the deck above.

'You look pale,' he commented, and with his gaze dropping to the glass of mineral water she was holding, 'And you haven't touched a drop of alcohol all night.'

She turned her head so that he wouldn't see the anguish in

her profile—the disturbing realisation that he had been watch-ing her—flinching as he added in an even more confidential voice, 'You aren't…pregnant by any chance?'

With her breath catching, Shannon swung to face him, her shoulder moving in the briefest of shrugs. 'Would it adhere more to your plans if I said I was?'

'Plans?' His eyes were dark with an emotion she couldn't fathom, but she could feel the tension in him, the anger he was doing his utmost to control.

'Sorry to disappoint you,' she murmured in an anguished whisper as someone descended the flybridge steps behind them—went below into the saloon—because wouldn't it make his position more secure, she agonised, if all he really wanted was the company and she was expecting his baby? 'Anyway,' she tagged on, struggling for something safer to say that wouldn't threaten to choke her, 'neither have you. Been drink-ing,' she clarified.

Apart from the caterers, for most of the evening he had been the only one without a glass in his hand. The impeccable host, self-restrained; self-disciplined; master of himself and of others.

'I like to stay in control,' he responded, confirming it, and with a harsher edge to his voice, 'But then you know that, don't you?' It was the first reference he had made to their confrontation back in London, to the accusation she had made and the awful row that had ensued.

'I only know you didn't deny it.'

'So therefore it must be true.'

She turned away so that he wouldn't see her tears reflected too clearly in the crimson of the setting sun.

'And yet you're still wearing my ring.' Quickly, she with-drew her hand from the rail, her fingers clenching against her middle. 'Is that for their benefit?' His chin jerked roughly upwards towards the flybridge, where most of the animated conversation was coming from. 'To save face?' he rasped. 'Or have you changed your mind about being engaged to a man who only wants you for what you're worth to him in stocks and shares?'

His hard derision flayed her and no less cruelly from wondering whether it was wholly justified.

'Do you?' she challenged, facing him squarely, her eyes fixing painfully on his.

But still his emotions remained shuttered beneath the concealing sweep of his thick lashes. 'You must make up your own mind about that.'

Her blue eyes clouding, tortured by doubts, silently she pleaded for reassurance.

'How can I?' she murmured, her throat constricted by emotion. She had trusted before, only to have that trust explode in her face. She couldn't go through it again.

But then someone called to him from the flybridge steps.

Aching with frustration, Shannon saw him glance over his shoulder, tension etching hard lines in his face as though he resented the intrusion as much as she did.

'We'll talk later,' he promised in a harsh whisper. But for now, his smile in place, he allowed himself to be drawn back into the party, leaving Shannon marvelling at how easily he could slip back into the role of urbane host, so that the middle-aged woman who was suddenly grabbing his attention could never have guessed at the seething complexity beneath that polished veneer.

Shannon didn't have another chance to speak to him alone until she was coming out of the guest cabin from the *en suite* much later. Not expecting anyone else to be below, she gasped as he emerged from the portside office cabin opposite, conscious of his hard masculinity dominating the cramped space at the foot of the stairs.

'You should have a glass of champagne. Settle those over-stretched nerves,' he commented drily, obviously noticing the way she flinched on seeing him. 'Either that or we'll have to find some other way to relax you.'

An insidious heat stole through her, making her throat dry, making her legs feel weak. 'You think you can get round me like that?'

He laughed softly. 'Can't I?'

Something throbbed at the very core of her femininity. 'No.'

'Well, we'll see later, shan't we?' Through the sounds of music, laughter and conversation above them, his voice was silkily seductive.

Images of the master suite flashed through her mind, the sensuality of the decor and its engulfing intimacy, the memory of mind-blowing passion, of pleasure, of her abandoned cries.

'That's what you think, Kane. And no doubt what my father's hoping.'

'One matter, then, on which I strongly applaud him.'

Accusation lit her eyes. 'Did you arrange this with him?'

'Did I heck!'

Strangely, she believed him. 'Just as well, then, that your efforts won't have been wasted,' she returned heatedly, 'because I'm driving back tonight!'

'Over my dead body!' All flippancy had gone out of him. His arm came up on the wall, trapping her there. She swallowed, hard, her pulses racing from his galvanising nearness, his evocative scent making her senses swim.

'Don't push me, Kane.'

He ignored her tremulous threat. 'Go in the morning, by all means,' he stated, as though it made little difference to him. 'But for heaven's sake, be sensible. Sober or not, in my opinion you aren't safe to be behind a wheel. You're tired. You're overwrought…'

'Who says I'm overwrought?' Even to her own ears, her voice sounded shrill with panic.

'Just listen to you. The only place for you is bed.'

'And that will solve everything, will it?' she breathed sarcastically, trying to deny the throbbing excitement his suggestion sent through her body even as her mind struggled to reject it.

'It will keep you off the road,' he told her, his face grim, 'because there's no way I'm letting you drive home tonight.'

'There's no way you can stop me!' she assured him resolutely, fearing he might try to. 'Unless you can give me one good reason that isn't about sex and my safety why I should stay.'

Her eyes locked with his and her throat clogged with something painfully acute as she saw the intensity of emotion in those steely irises. Desire, that was all it was, she managed to convince herself. Raw need, driving and very powerful, but which still only amounted to a devastating physical attraction which, if she stayed, she would only succumb to, she realised hopelessly. She longed to give in to her own insatiable need for him, lose herself again in their unbelievable lovemaking. But then she would never know. Never be sure...

Kane started to speak, but broke off, glancing up. Someone was waiting at the top of the stairs to use the *en suite*.

Grabbing the opportunity to tear herself away, Shannon raced upstairs and left him standing there—letting the woman through—wondering what it was he had been about to say.

It was after eleven before most of the guests started to depart, but at last only a few remained.

The night air was cool, but Shannon remained on the upper deck, unconsciously rubbing her arms as she stared out across the night-shrouded marina, glad of a few moments alone.

'So here you are.'

The familiar deep voice made her back ramrod-straight. *Kane!* His footsteps were ominously light over the teak-laid deck.

'I just wanted to thank you for coming.' His tone was gentle, like the occasional rippling of the water against the hull. 'It went very well.'

'Yes.' Laughter drifted up to them from the aft, from the stragglers of the party. 'But it wasn't my decision,' she repeated in response to what he had said about her being there. 'My father insisted on it.'

She heard the sharp breath he took. 'Is that the only reason you came?'

She glanced at him over her shoulder, standing but a few feet away. Engulfed by the night, his features were in shadow, but his voice was roughened by an emotion as tangible as the cool wind that was lifting his hair, making her shiver so that she rubbed her bare arms again to try and keep them warm.

'You know, for someone who's so together in most ways,' he murmured in a softly mocking tone, 'you're never adequately prepared for the weather.'

She gave a small gasp from something suddenly being placed around her shoulders, the black silk bolero she had left down in the saloon.

'Thanks,' she breathed, willing herself to move away from him, but his hands closed over her upper arms, restraining her, the arm across her back half-turning her into him.

'What does this remind you of?'

'Don't,' she protested, because she knew too well. That night in Cannes when he had slipped his jacket around her on the promenade and they had come back here alone, hungry, desperate for each other...

'You're trembling,' he whispered, inhaling the perfume of her hair. 'Because you want this. We both want this...'

'Don't,' she repeated breathlessly, panicking because he was right.

'Why?' he asked hoarsely. 'Because you're still prepared to believe what your father told you? That I'm marrying you for every reason except the obvious? Because you can't imagine I could possibly be in love with you?' That raw edge to his voice had her looking at him questioningly, aching to believe it, her dizzying senses straining towards his warmth, the scent of his cologne, his nearness stripping the last shred of her resistance so that she would have moved into his arms if he hadn't stepped quickly away.

'Ah, here she is!' The middle-aged couple who had accompanied him from Guernsey were suddenly joining them on the deck. 'We're going now, Kane.' Hands were shaken and thanks offered for a marvellous day afloat; a splendid evening. 'I'm looking for a Porsche,' the woman told him, 'and Shannon just happened to mention that she's selling hers and that it's in the car park, so we're going over there now to have a look at it before our taxi arrives. Great boat,' she enthused with a last glance around her, and then with a knowing look at Shannon that strayed appreciatively to Kane, 'Made for romance. Come on, then, dear.' Already she was urging her indulgently smiling husband back down the steps. 'Let's take a look at this car.'

Following, about to descend after them, Shannon gasped from the sudden, iron-like clasp on her arm.

'You didn't tell me you were selling your car.' His eyes searched her face, while the light from the deck below made him look strangely lined and tired.

'Didn't I?' It came out as a croak. *Please don't look at me like that!*

'And after you've shown them the Porsche…you're coming back?'

Those harrowed words—the tremor in his voice—caused her to hesitate. 'No.' Somehow she managed to get it out, her voice faltering as she went on, 'Well, you said yourself, the company's healthy and the new man will do a great job following your policies.' Her tongue seemed to cleave to her mouth, the words she had rehearsed and which she had thought would be so easy to say seeming to stick in her throat, but somehow she forced them past her lips. 'I'm going back to Peru.'

Was that anguish in his face? Was she really doing this to him when every part of her wanted to tell him that it wasn't true? That she wanted to stay? Soothe the pain away and have him look at her again with that old, familiar smile? But she'd told the others she would show them her car. She had responsibilities. So did he.

'I've got to go.'

The next instant she was tearing away from him, down the steps to the aft without a backward glance, the sound of his agonised, 'Shannon!' ripping through her heart before she made light work of the second flight of steps and jumped quickly ashore to join the others.

CHAPTER TWELVE

IN THE dark interior of the Porsche—silent now that the couple had gone—Shannon sat back on her seat, and closed her eyes.

They had decided not to buy it in the end—something about buying a four-by-four for their three dogs—and, friendly though they were, she was glad to be alone so that at last she could have a chance to think.

She had told Kane she was driving back tonight. But how could she go? she berated herself. He had said he wanted to talk to her, and whatever he had to say she wanted to listen to him, she realised achingly.

He had said he loved her. Hot tears pressed out from under her closed eyelids. Well, almost, she corrected silently. But how could a man who treated her with so much tenderness be anything else but in love? No matter what Ranulph had said.

Perhaps he had meant well, she tried to compromise as she thought back to that awful moment when her father had told her what Kane stood to gain out of their marriage. But all her life she had known that Ranulph's tact, understanding and sensitivity towards others had been questionable at the very least—towards his staff, towards her mother, towards her. Only Kane had ever really generated any respect in him. He was probably the type of man that Ranulph would have wanted to call a son—the heir he had always wanted—she considered now, while she had been a mere girl, discounted, overindulged in compensation for the lack of parental love; attention-seeking. Her character had been forged first by loneliness and then betrayal and then, latterly, over the past couple of years, by seeing life at its cruellest and at its most humane. But she wasn't nineteen any more. She had done a lot of growing up in the past three years. She was a woman now—in control of her own destiny, her own life.

Heaven only knew, she was no angel. But she did have some good points, and one was the ability to make judgements for herself. And from every word and gesture that Kane had made tonight—from the harrowing anguish in his eyes whenever he looked at her, to that last note of unmistakable pain in his voice when he had called her name—every instinct told her not to doubt this man.

Her pulse was throbbing with an intensity of purpose as she stepped out into the darkness, and depressed the remote control button that locked the Porsche.

From his seat on the upper-helm deck, Kane wished the final couple would go.

It was just his luck, he decided with growing impatience and a twinge of conscience for thinking it, that the last guests to linger should be a pair of boating enthusiasts! Interesting though they were, it didn't alter the fact that he had had a long day and a decidedly longer and more harrowing evening, so much so that he didn't know how much longer he could sit there playing the responsive and amiable host.

Ever since Shannon had left, going off with that other couple, he hadn't been able to keep his mind on a thing. He'd thought, during those last moments, that if he could have got her on her own long enough, he might have been able to persuade her to stay. He could almost have believed she'd wanted to, but then they had been interrupted, and she'd gone, and much as he had wanted to go after her he'd had to stay and attend to his other guests. He'd half-hoped that she'd come back. No, that wasn't right, he corrected himself with a mental grimace. He'd darn well prayed that she would! Only she hadn't.

If he had had his car, he thought now, and he'd been alone, he would have chased after her—caught up with her if he had had to break every speed limit to do it. But he wasn't alone and he didn't have his car, and the internal flight he'd booked back to London wasn't leaving until tomorrow, which left him aching with frustration at every turn.

It didn't help, either, to keep on reminding himself that it was all his own fault for not telling her the full facts in the beginning, letting her know about the proposal her father had put to him. She'd been let down badly by a man before. He should have made allowances for that, he berated himself, instead of storming off as he had last Monday. It was only natural that she'd find it hard to trust... Mechanically he nodded at something the other man was saying, made some reply and hoped he was producing the right responses. He'd just never thought that Ranulph would actually tell her...

Shannon could hear voices on the upper deck. They belonged to the couple who had said they'd sailed round India or somewhere and Kane, whose brief, urbane responses to whatever they were saying, were none the less laced with definite undertones of tension.

She wanted to go up and see him, she thought, aching with longing—let him know she had come back. But she probably looked dreadful with her make-up smudged and her face blotchy from crying, she suspected, deciding against it. Apart from which, she didn't want to face anyone but Kane again tonight.

All the lights were on as she stepped into the welcoming luxury of the saloon. Everyone else had gone, she was relieved to see. A sound, however, drew her attention to the cabin area down beyond the galley.

The last of the caterers leaving, she realised, recognising the man coming up the stairs.

Not wishing to be seen, quickly Shannon slipped behind the partition and down the rear stairs to the private suite.

The room was as she remembered it, the memory of that night in Cannes leaping out at her from the black and gold furnishings, the soft lighting and the understated mirror over the big bed.

She had fallen in love with him irrevocably that night. On this yacht. In this room. In this bed. And even as she lay there, telling him her most intimate secrets, she had known with all her woman's intuition that he would never hurt her. Use her. Betray her. She had been a fool to allow anyone else to make her think he would.

She'd wait for him here, she decided with pulse-throbbing anticipation. Make herself look more presentable. Tell him she was sorry not to have trusted him. And then…

If he forgives you.

She was halfway through the door of the *en suite* when the nasty little thought accosted her. Of course. There had been times tonight when he had appeared so cold. But what did she expect? she asked herself. It wasn't a very nice thing she had accused him of. But what if she had misread the signs? Misinterpreted his words? Set too much store on automatically assuming he would forgive her? Take her back? What if he didn't even like her any more?

Her perfume seemed to haunt him as he came down the stairs.

Amarige. He would know it anywhere. But surely, if she had used the master suite while she had been on board, her perfume wouldn't still be lingering quite so strongly.

In which case this aching torment must be driving him mad, Kane despaired, opening the small door on the stairs outside the main cabin, because his last guests certainly were. The woman had made noises to her husband about leaving over half an hour ago, and now the man was asking to see the engine room!

With that over with, as the other man went ahead of him, back up the stairs, Kane hesitated outside his cabin door.

Her perfume was as strong as ever. And was that a tap running? he wondered, listening, every nerve pumping, every sense alert.

Why had she come back? Had she forgotten something? he tried analysing chaotically. Or had she decided she wanted to talk this thing through after all? But why hadn't she come up to find him? Suppose she had only come back for a show-down? Only to let him know how low she thought he was and then leave again? He wanted to fling open the door and find out. Go in there, drag her into his arms and drug her senseless with his kisses until she was so weak with desire she wouldn't have any choice but to listen to him. He didn't know what stopped him. Only, he supposed, these guests he still had to deal with. Grimly, he reminded himself of his duty as their unfailing host.

But in the meantime, suppose Shannon got tired of waiting before he could free himself of his responsibilities? Decided that he wasn't worth even a showdown after all, and simply left?

He'd never felt so out of control in his life. Which was pretty paradoxical, he thought, when the problem breaking them up was what all this had been over! Power. That was what she'd called it, wasn't it? As if he was some sort of control freak!

Although…

As he turned back up the stairs, his mouth took on a rather ironic curve.

There were just times when you had to exercise some.

The throb of the engine brought Shannon's head up in front of the *en suite* mirror. The hair she had been brushing forward was tossed wildly back, framing her head and shoulders like a shimmering aura.

What was Kane doing?

She ran into the bedroom, her brush still in her hand.

He was taking the boat out! The receding lights of the shore through the large oval portholes confirmed it. Why? Where was he going?

She had heard the last two guests leave a short time ago; had been expecting him to put in an appearance—come down to the cabin. He obviously wasn't taking anyone else for a moonlit cruise. And he was flying back to London in the morning. So why had he left the marina?

Carelessly, she threw her brush down onto the bed. Time, she decided, with a little tingle of nerves, to let him know she was there!

Tripping over to the door, she found it wouldn't open. Why wouldn't it open? she wondered, baffled. And after several further futile attempts, it dawned. Kane must have come down while she had been applying fresh make-up—trying to make herself look presentable—and she hadn't heard him. He had known she was down here and he had locked her in!

Rebellion vied with a wild excitement. What did he think he was doing? Taking seriously the suggestion he'd told her Bart had made to him that day in St Tropez about locking her up?

A feverish little gasp escaped her. He wouldn't even have entertained the idea if he'd still been angry with her, she grasped immediately. He'd only dare to do this if he was hopelessly—crazily—in love with her. If he realised, as he had to, she thought with her blood racing, that she was hopelessly—crazily—in love with him!

Unless he was planning to sink the yacht with her in it, or toss her over the side, she thought with a galvanised little laugh, what was he intending to do with her? Anticipation was a pulsing heat in her veins, because she knew very well.

Perhaps he thought kidnapping her was the only way to get her back in his bed—make her listen to him, she thought. And she would listen to everything he had to say. But right now the last thing she wanted to do with him was talk!

So what was she supposed to do in the meantime? Just sit and wait?

It felt like a challenge for supremacy—or equality—even if it wasn't. And if it was, she thought, did he imagine she wouldn't rise to it?

Apart from which, she'd never just sat and waited for anything in her life.

OK, Kane Falconer...

With lip-biting excitement she glanced around her and made a swift assessment of the cabin. Then, purposefully, she lifted her arms and peeled off the tight, confining dress.

Agile as a cat, Shannon pushed up the upholstered seat above the escape hatch and stepped nimbly out onto the aft.

Behind her, over the dark water, the boat's wake bubbled like a white cloud. Overhead the sunroof of the canopy was still open and the midnight sky was dusted with a million stars.

Out here at sea, in little more than her black satin basque bra, and French knickers, the night air felt cool against her skin, but a feverish anticipation kept her warm.

The little lights beneath each step guided her way to the flybridge. The wind lifted her hair and she could feel her pulses pumping, but her black-stockinged feet made no sound on the teak-laid steps.

Kane was standing at the helm with his back to her, the sight of his achingly dear figure and his dark head—bent in concentration as he did something on the instrument panel—causing an almost painful constriction in her throat.

How could she ever have doubted him? The love she felt for him was overwhelming as she watched him glance towards the lights that winked along the coast then drop down onto the seat, check something on one of the monitors, reduce the speed of knots.

They were slowing down.

With feline stealth, Shannon slid around the barbecue, crept up behind him and, silent as a shadow, lifted her arms and clamped her hands over his eyes. She heard his breath catch, felt his back stiffen, but he made no other sound or movement as she breathed huskily against his hair-roughened jaw, 'I want to take you to bed.'

But then, swift as lightning, he was reaching round and pulling her down across his lap, and nothing mattered because she was where she belonged—locked in those powerful arms while she responded to his devouring kisses as though she had been parted from him for a lifetime.

'What made you come back?' The words were raggedly spoken when he eventually lifted his head.

'You did.'

'I did?'

'Oh, Kane! I've been such a fool! I'm so sorry for all the things I said—accusing you of marrying me just to get control of the company. I know you love me.' And rather desperately, 'You do love me, don't you?'

His lips—like his voice—were tender against her throat. 'How could you ever have doubted it?'

Wasn't that what she had asked herself only moments before?

'I guess I've wanted you for so long, I couldn't believe I could really be that lucky,' she murmured.

'Oh, I'm the lucky one,' he breathed. 'When I thought you'd left me tonight, I was going out of my mind!'

'So was I. That's why I had to come back.' His hair beneath her fingers was thick and strong, and caressingly she drew them along the rough line of his jaw, tracing the curve of his wonderfully warm mouth to the tantalising cleft in his chin. 'And then you locked me in!' The knowledge that he would go to such lengths made her slightly breathless. 'Kidnapped me!'

'Only because I was desperate to talk to you.' He leaned across her to do something on the dashboard. The yacht was doing little more than drifting now. 'I had to keep you on board until the others got off. And I brought us out here because I wasn't prepared to take any chances on having another row and one of us walking off again.' His words were a painful reminder of the torment she had suffered over the past week after he had walked out on her, and then the unnecessary anguish that she must have put him through tonight.

'I won't leave you,' she whispered, lifting her red lips to his, and was disappointed when his mouth lightly brushed the corner of hers without actually granting more of the kisses she craved.

'Later,' he promised teasingly, on hearing her little murmur of frustration. 'But first there are just one or two things I want you to know.'

His hand was sliding along her silkily clad leg, over the cool, smooth flesh between her stocking-top and her panties. He wasn't sure how he was going to keep his mind on what he wanted to say to her, but he was going to try.

'I'm sorry I stormed off the way I did on Monday, but I was just so hurt—so angry. With you. With Ranulph.' Shannon could still detect an element of annoyance in the way he breathed her father's name. 'When he approached me and asked for my help, I did it initially purely for my own interests. The shares were low. I could afford to buy a lot. The aim was to stay there for a year and turn things round. Then sell again to reinvest in one of my own ventures. When your father asked me to find you—offered to sell me the controlling share if I not only brought you back, but also actually *married* you—I as good as laughed his proposal out of the window. There was no way I was going to agree to a thing like that. I think, in some ways, Ranulph's still living in the nineteenth century—thinking he can pick the man his daughter should marry.

'I started looking for you because, as I told you before, I could see how much he wanted you back, but the main reason was because I was worried about you. I wanted to see you again and I needed to find out for myself where and how you were. When I found you in Barcelona that day, it was pure coincidence, but what your father had said had been said. There was no way that that could be retracted. It came back to me loud and clear, that night I proposed. But there was no way I could have you alone on this boat without falling in love with you. I'd always known you were an enchantress. I just wasn't prepared for just how devastating your effect on me would be. When we got engaged, I decided that if your father wanted to see it his way—that I was going along with his original proposal—then that was entirely up to him. What I hadn't reckoned on was that he'd be insensitive enough to tell you about it.' Again, that edge of anger was apparent in his voice. 'I wondered if I should have told you myself, but that still wouldn't have been proof that I wasn't the ruthless power-seeker you finally suspected me of being. I was in a totally no-win situation. All I could do was hope you'd realise my strengths and weaknesses for yourself.'

'I do,' Shannon uttered, all her love and tenderness and desire for him bubbling over inside her. She ran a loving finger along his jaw line, down the corded length of his throat, and heard him catch his breath when her hand slid beneath his shirt to caress the warm satin of his shoulder. 'Except that you don't have many weaknesses.'

He laughed softly. 'Well…maybe just one…' The masculine hand that slid beneath the lace edging of her panties drew a guttural sob of pleasure from her. 'Seriously…' A breath filled his lungs as he dragged himself back from the precipice of need. There was still something he needed to tell her; something over which he couldn't yet let desire ride, because she had to know. 'When we're married, I'm going to have that controlling interest, Shannon.'

The golden lashes that lay against the wells of her eyes flickered open. For a second a small crease marred the smooth curvature of her forehead.

'I'm going to have those controlling shares—and I'm going to be making them over to you. That way you'll always have a say in how things are done—with proposals you want to put forward.'

'Oh, Kane!' Tears filling her eyes, she sat up and hugged him, revelling in his warmth and strength and the intensity of love she could see deep in his eyes. 'I love you,' she murmured. 'I've always loved you. And you've given me so much. And all I've ever been thought of until now was wayward and rebellious...'

'Mmm.' He sounded as though he not only agreed but also rather liked the idea, and held her away from him so that he could look at her.

Drily, he said, 'I thought I locked you in your room. How did you get out?'

A delicious little *frisson* ran through her. With eyes twinkling she breathed sultrily, 'You knew I would!'

His febrile gaze ran over the basque, above which the soft swell of her breasts protruded, his hand shaping the bodice where it nipped her slender waist.

'I'm glad you did,' he approved, fingers sliding over the silkier fabric spanning her hip to the tantalising lace above her stocking top. Almost he wished that he'd left the yacht back there in the marina. At least they would still be moored now...

'Well, I couldn't go climbing onto the vanity unit and through the escape hatch with that tight dress on, could I?' she purred, sounding pleased with herself.

'Definitely not,' he agreed in a deep, appreciative tone. Pulling her down onto his lap again, so that her hair was draped over his arm, he wondered what he had done to steal the heart of such a wonderfully warm, loving and generous woman. The scar on her forehead, he noticed, had faded now—faded like her doubts, and there was a healthy glow about her that hadn't been there when he had first found her.

'You're beautiful,' he whispered hoarsely, unable to get enough of her visual loveliness. 'Beautiful and clever and...' he slipped a finger under one of her suspenders and tweaked it playfully '...outrageous. Even as a child you were outrageous,' he remembered, his voice thickening with emotion.

'I wasn't a child—I was a woman,' she reminded him, recalling the futile longing of those days. 'But you never noticed.'

'Oh, I noticed,' he breathed huskily, surprising her, but she couldn't answer him because of the sensation of his warm hand moving over her body and she gasped as it closed over the soft roundedness of her breast. 'As I said, outrageous, rebellious, unbelievably sexy...'

She groaned from all that he was doing to her, moving restlessly against him on his lap.

'And very, *very* attention-seeking,' she reminded him imperatively, sliding an arm around his neck to draw him down to her—put her out of her misery.

And, needing no more encouragement, he dipped his head to give her all the attention she wanted, because there was nothing left to say.

REQUEST YOUR FREE BOOKS!

2 FREE NOVELS
PLUS 2
FREE GIFTS!

From the magnificent Blue Palace to the wild
plains of the desert, be swept away as three
sheikh princes find their brides.

Proud and passionate…
Three billionaires are soon to discover
the truth to their ancestry…

Wild and untamed…
They are all heirs to the throne of
the desert kingdom of Kharastan…

*Though royalty is their destiny, these sheikhs
are as untamed as their homeland!*

Don't miss any of the books
in this brand-new trilogy from

Sharon Kendrick!

THE SHEIKH'S ENGLISH BRIDE,
Book #2612, Available March 2007

THE SHEIKH'S UNWILLING WIFE,
Book #2620, Available April 2007

THE DESERT KING'S VIRGIN BRIDE,
Book #2628, Available May 2007

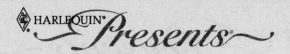

Coming Next Month

#2611 ROYALLY BEDDED, REGALLY WEDDED Julia James
By Royal Command
Lizzy Mitchell is an ordinary girl, but she has something Prince Rico Renaldi wants: the heir to the throne of his principality! Lizzy is the heir's adoptive mother, and she will do anything to keep her son. Then Rico demands a marriage of convenience....

#2612 THE SHEIKH'S ENGLISH BRIDE Sharon Kendrick
The Desert Princes
When billionaire Xavier de Maistre discovers he could inherit the kingdom of Kharastan, it's a surprise. But more surprising is Laura Cottingham, the lawyer who delivered the news. Xavier wants her, but is she ready to be tamed and tempted by this desert prince?

#2613 THE ITALIAN BOSS'S SECRETARY MISTRESS Cathy Williams
Mistress to a Millionaire
Rose is in love with her gorgeous boss, Gabriel Gessi, but her resolve to forget him crumbles when he demands they work closely together...on a Caribbean island! She knows the sexy Italian is the master of persuasion, and it won't be long before he's added her to his agenda.

#2614 THE KOUVARIS MARRIAGE Diana Hamilton
Wedlocked!
Madeleine is devastated to learn that her gorgeous Greek billionaire husband, Dimitri Kouvaris, only married her to conceive a child! She begs for divorce, but Dimitri is determined to keep Maddie at his side—and in his bed—until she bears the Kouvaris heir.

#2615 THE PRINCE'S CONVENIENT BRIDE Robyn Donald
The Royal House of Illyria
Prince Marco Considine knows he's met his match when he meets model Jacoba Sinclair. But Jacoba has a secret: she is Illyrian, just like Prince Marco, a fact that could endanger her life. Marco seizes a perfect opportunity to protect her—by announcing their engagement!

#2616 WANTED: MISTRESS AND MOTHER Carol Marinelli
Ruthless!
Ruthless barrister Dante Costello hires Matilda Hamilton to help his troubled little girl. An intense attraction flares between them, and Dante decides he will offer Matilda the position of mistress. But what Dante thought was lust turns out to be something far greater.

#2617 THE SPANIARD'S MARRIAGE DEMAND Maggie Cox
A Mediterranean Marriage
Leandro Reyes could have any girl he wanted. Only in the cold light of morning did Isabella realize she was just another notch on his belt. But their passionate night together was to have a lasting consequence Leandro couldn't ignore. His solution: to demand that Isabella marry him!

#2618 THE CARLOTTA DIAMOND Lee Wilkinson
Dinner at 8
Charlotte Christie had no idea that the priceless diamond necklace she wore on her wedding day meant more than she realized. But Simon Farringdon didn't see her innocence until too late. What would happen when Charlotte discovered the Carlotta Diamond was his only motive for marriage?

HPCNM0207